A Fate Worse Than Dragons

JOHN MOORE

ACE BOOKS, NEW YORK

THE BERKLEY PUBLISHING GROUP
Published by the Penguin Group
Penguin Group (USA) Inc.
375 Hudson Street, New York, New York 10014, USA
Penguin Group (Canada), 90 Eglinton Avenue East, Suite 700, Toronto, Ontario M4P 2Y3, Canada
(a division of Pearson Penguin Canada Inc.)
Penguin Books Ltd., 80 Strand, London WC2R 0RL, England
Penguin Group Ireland, 25 St. Stephen's Green, Dublin 2, Ireland (a division of Penguin Books Ltd.)
Penguin Group (Australia), 250 Camberwell Road, Camberwell, Victoria 3124, Australia
(a division of Pearson Australia Group Pty. Ltd.)
Penguin Books India Pvt. Ltd., 11 Community Centre, Panchsheel Park, New Delhi—110 017, India
Penguin Group (NZ), 67 Apollo Drive, Mairangi Bay, Auckland 1311, New Zealand
(a division of Pearson New Zealand Ltd.)
Penguin Books (South Africa) (Pty.) Ltd., 24 Sturdee Avenue, Rosebank, Johannesburg 2196,
South Africa

Penguin Books Ltd., Registered Offices: 80 Strand, London WC2R 0RL, England

A FATE WORSE THAN DRAGONS

An Ace Book / published by arrangement with the author

Copyright © 2007 by John Moore.
Cover art by Walter Velez.
Cover design by Annette Fiore.
Interior text design by Kristin del Rosario.

ISBN: 978-0-7394-8345-9

ACE
Ace Books are published by The Berkley Publishing Group,
a division of Penguin Group (USA) Inc.,
375 Hudson Street, New York, New York 10014.
ACE and the "A" design are trademarks belonging to Penguin Group (USA) Inc.

PRINTED IN THE UNITED STATES OF AMERICA

To Ashley. To Colleen. To Morgan. To Linda and Juli and Rhonda and Kathy. And to Dusty and Renee and . . . well, actually to all the women who asked me, "Why is the redhead always the bad girl in your stories? Why don't you write a story where the redhead is the good girl?"

This isn't it.

This is the forest primeval, where the mur-muring pines and hemlocks, bearded with moss, stand like Druids of eld, and the young elms sway like sailors in the eleventh hour of a twelve-hour liberty. This is the forest primeval, where golden eyes and white fangs flash silently in the ever-present twilight, and the roe startles and leaps at a rustle in the dry leaves. This is the forest primeval, where it is lunchtime.

In fact, it's pretty much always lunchtime in the forest primeval, or even in the forest contemporary, which makes more use of open space and natural light and attracts a younger crowd of predators. There are always big carnivores looking for meals, although some are more finicky than others. Wolves and bears will happily feast on a dead carcass, but the lion and the panther like to kill their own dinner. Dragons, too, prefer fresh meat. And they like it roasted.

There was a very slight movement at the edge of the

forest. Terry thought it could have been a dragon. It was hard to see. The sun was high and bright, and the distant trees cast deep shadows. The leaves had already turned color. In another month the woods would be bare of leaves, but now the foliage was still thick on the trees, and the shadows beneath those trees were dark enough to conceal something big, and the birds in those trees had suddenly become silent. That hinted at the presence of a predator, and not in a subtle way, either. These birds not only refused to sing, they were ready to swear that they had been on the opposite side of the forest on this particular day and had five friends to vouch for them. Away from the trees, in the center of the meadow, a skinned goat sizzled on a spit. Beneath it, a small fire was steadily burning down to coals. On his own side of the meadow, Terry held his lance steady and peered through the trunks, keeping his horse away from the open space and out of sight.

A stout man in a rough leather jerkin was standing at the head of the horse, one hand resting on the bridle, the other holding a bottle with a garishly printed label. "It's not coming," he said. "The mix is all wrong, I tell you. Rosemary and mint, that's what we should have used. It's a well-known recipe."

"That's for lamb, Huggins. This is a goat," said the young man in the saddle. "This is the recipe we want. Besides, those are magical herbs out there. I bought that seasoning from a first-rate magician. He said dragons go crazy for it."

Huggins read the label on the empty bottle: SIZZLIN' SORCERER BARBECUE SAUCE—OLD FAMILY RECIPE. "Sure." He tossed the bottle away. Then he slipped a few paces back, behind the horse, out of Terry's line of sight, removed a tin flask from a pocket of his jerkin, extracted the cork, and took a hefty swallow. "I was thinking, Sire," he said. "I was wondering if perhaps you could give me my wages along about now."

Terry kept his eyes fixed on the woods. The motion he thought he saw had not reappeared. "Huggins, you know there's no money until the rents come due. Then I'll pay you. Have I ever failed to pay you?"

"No, Sire." Huggins had the kind of round, jovial face that inspires immediate confidence in young children and none at all in adults. "But then, suppose—just suppose— something was to happen to you, say, on the way home. *After* you slay this dragon. Perhaps you fall ill, let's say. I'm sure you wouldn't want to leave me financially strained."

Again there was a flicker of movement among the trees. Terry narrowed his eyes. "Huggins, this unusual concern with my well-being transmits a certain air of in-security. Am I to infer that my faithful squire lacks faith in my abilities?"

"Not at all, Sire, not at all," his faithful squire assured him. "You can count on my steadfast loyalty, Sire. If you say you can slay a dragon, I do not doubt you. But then, I expect the other nine knights also had faith in their own abilities. And they . . ."

"They had squires who stayed sober."

"Just a little nip to steady my nerves, Sire."

"By now your nerves should be steady enough to sup-port a billiard table. Put the flask away. And throw some more water on the horse."

Huggins dipped a bucket into a shallow stream and splashed water on Terry. The knight wore armor, but the armor was covered with wet blankets. "On the horse, Huggins." The horse was draped with blankets also, brown and gray wool to fit in among the trees. But you couldn't cover the legs, not if you wanted to get up any speed, and Terry knew the horse was not going to survive this day. It shifted its feet, showing its nervousness. Terry patted it on the neck and murmured calming words. Other knights had told him they talked to their horses, soothing the animals, encouraging them before battle, with good results. Terry's horse rolled its eyes every time he spoke to it, although it was impossible for him to tell if this meant the horse was afraid or if it thought Terry was an idiot. He gave up, and said aloud, "Nine knights in ten years. That's really not too bad for a dragon this size. It's fewer than one per year."

"It's a hundred percent casualty rate, Sire. In the great and honorable game of knights against dragons, this one is an undefeated champion. You know, Sire?" Huggins went on, as if the thought had just occurred to him. "We can still turn and walk away from this. There's no shame in it. No one back home knows we came down here."

"We can't go back without trying, Huggins. We have our responsibilities. This dragon has been terrorizing the locals for a decade. These honest, hardworking peasants, slaving away in the fields, those innocent young children, cowering in their hovels, all of them living in fear, never knowing if the next moment might bring the dreaded . . ."

"You never worried about the peasants before, Sire."

"The reward wasn't big enough then."

"What reward? You mean the bounty? It still isn't very big. Wait for a while. Let it kill a few more knights, and they might start offering real money."

"Not the bounty, Huggins. There is another reward. The real reward. The hand of the princess in marriage."

This time both his squire and his horse rolled their eyes. Huggins offered up his flask. "Take a drink, Sire. Maybe it will clear your head. If this is about some girl . . ."

"Put it away, Huggins. *Now.* And it's not *some girl*, it's the most wonderful girl in the kingdom. The most beautiful, adorable, delightful girl in *all* the Twenty Kingdoms. The sweetest, the fairest, the most charming . . . um . . . graceful . . . let's see . . ."

"Winsome," Huggins suggested.

"Win some, lose some, this is no time for philosophy. The princess—whoa! There it is!"

Huggins snapped the flask away from his lips. He ran forward, almost to the edge of the meadow, looked out, and immediately backed up. "Son of a bitch!" He tried to jam the flask into his belt, found as usual that a roll of fat prevented this, and fumbled it into the pocket of his jerkin. He grabbed the bucket and began furiously splashing water on Terry.

Terry watched the dragon. It was a normal-sized dragon, which meant it was pretty damn big. Its shoulders stood as high as the horse, and the body was twice as long. The menacing tail added more to the length. It seemed to be made entirely of teeth, claws, and muscle covered with thick scales. It had emerged from the cover of the wood, but was still cautious about going into the meadow, sniffing the air, stalking back and forth along the tree line, turning its head to look at the roasting goat from one side, then the other. A few drops of saliva ran down one side of its mouth. A thin tendril of smoke drifted from the other side.

A face full of water obscured Terry's view.

He pushed up his visor to wipe his eyes. "That's enough, Huggins. We're wet already. Why are you acting so surprised? We've been stalking this thing for three weeks. Get a grip, man."

"Yes, Sire. You *said* you were tracking it." The squire already had another bucket of water. He turned around, looking for something else to throw it on. "But in all honesty, Sire, your skills as a tracker aren't worth spit. Mostly you were just riding around and asking people if they'd seen a dragon lately. And they always said yes. And then they sent us to some god-awful swamp or briar patch, or up some cliff. I thought they were just having you on."

"You're not a trusting soul, are you, Huggins?" The knight spoke without taking his eyes off the dragon. It stopped moving and stared intently at the roasting goat. Fat dripped into the fire, causing tendrils of flame to lick at the meat. A puff of fragrant smoke reached the animal's nostrils. The dragon began slavering. Strings of drool extended from its jaws. It was a thoroughly disgusting sight, but Terry smiled. He had the beast locked in now. It wasn't going to leave without its dinner.

"Huggins!" he said sharply. His squire had been staring at the dragon with horrified fascination and slowly backing away. "Get the hammer and the horse spike!"

Huggins snapped back to reality. He rummaged in the duffel bags until he came up with a mallet and thick spike. He held them up for Terry's inspection.

Terry nodded. "Huggins, this horse is going to be injured. I don't want it to suffer. As soon as you can approach safely, put the horse out of its misery. Do this even before you attend to me. Got it?" Huggins nodded, wide-eyed. Before he could say anything, the dragon charged.

A flock of grouse erupted from the field. Terry snapped down his visor, gripped his lance more tightly, and leaned forward in the saddle. *Wait for it, wait for it,* he told himself. Dragons were fast. They could outrun a horse on level ground. *Let him get the goat. Let him get distracted.* The beast was almost at the goat before Terry gave his horse the spurs.

His visor narrowed his field of vision to a bright band of meadow, sunlight, and scaly beast. It reached the goat. Terry heard quite clearly the crunch of teeth through the ribs. Then the only sound seemed to be the thunder of hooves. The dragon grew larger and larger in his vision. It hunkered down over the goat, and Terry aimed the iron-tipped lance at a spot between the shoulder and the neck. He'd been told that if you could get the point through the scales, and if you missed the shoulder bones, you could drive the lance right through to the heart. Then the dragon lifted its head, and Terry switched his aim to the throat. The books all said that the scales were thinner here, and you could get a killing blow to the neck. Then the dragon saw Terry.

Swallow, thought Terry. *Swallow, damn you.* The dragon had the goat hanging out of both sides of its jaws. If it swallowed, the goat would be in its throat, and Terry would have extra precious moments before the dragon could spew flame.

Regrettably, he was up against a dragon with a strong work ethic, the kind that knew business came first. It dropped the goat on the ground, spread its jaws wide, and roared.

The horse almost turned aside, and that was very nearly the end of it, but it was a good horse and responded well to pressure from Terry's knees and his hand on its neck. It lowered its head and charged faster. The dragon stood its ground. Terry aimed his lance at the open mouth. And the dragon flamed him.

It seemed to happen instantly. One moment he was staring at an incredible number of incredibly large and crooked teeth. In the next moment he was engulfed in fire. Every inch of his skin suddenly felt like it had been burned raw and dipped in salt water. An instant later the pain filled his lungs. The dragon disappeared behind a wall of bright orange. The horse screamed and stumbled. Terry felt his lance strike something hard. He tried to hold on to it, but the horse fell from beneath him, and he was lifted up and flung away. The orange light vanished. He had a brief glimpse of blue sky. He had a briefer glimpse of tan grass. He got a good long view of blackness.

When he came back to consciousness he was looking at a circle of concerned faces. Someone had removed his helmet. Cool air was blowing across his skin. He greeted them with a paroxysm of prolonged coughing, which they seemed to find reassuring, as the oldest man turned around, and shouted, "He's alive!" Terry heard cheering. There were people streaming across the field—local villagers—Terry recognized some of them from his visit yesterday. Eager hands helped him to his feet.

"Name's Brimble," said the oldest man. He was portly, with a neatly trimmed white beard. "I'm the mayor of Dasgut Village. I believe you stayed at my inn yesterday. Take it easy now, son. It tossed you a pretty fair distance."

Terry got his coughing under control. "Is it dead?" He looked around, but saw no sign of the dragon. Huggins, on the other hand, was coming across the meadow.

"Dead, dead, dead. Yes, sir. We found it in the woods with a lance through its head. A very professional job, through the roof of the mouth and into the skull, just like the books said. You have a nice little bounty coming to you, good Sir Knight. Come on back to my inn, and I'll get the paperwork going. This is a joyous day for us. For years that dragon has forced us to lock ourselves in our homes. And only eat boiled meat."

Someone got the idea of ringing the church bell. More people were streaming across the meadow from the direction of the village. Others were coming in from the fields. There were even a couple of soldiers on horseback.

"I've already sent a messenger to the king. He'll be very pleased. He's been waiting a long time for something like this to happen." Brimble winked. "I'm sure that as soon as he hears about it, he'll be running to his daughter with the good news."

The crowd of people grew, gathering around the two of them with interest and awe. Little children ran out of wattle-and-thatch homes, joined the crowd, and squirmed their way to the front. Terry recognized that a theatrical gesture was called for. He stood up straight. His body felt like one large bruise, but he did his best to strike a noble pose. "And I shall be running to her side," he declaimed, placing a hand on his chest. "For although the hand of the princess is now mine, my heart shall forever belong to her. My passion burns like the flame of that dragon, my thoughts are with her always. Inseparable, united by love, the beautiful Princess Gloria and I will never part . . ."

"Jane," interrupted Brimble.

"What?"

"Princess Jane, good Sir Knight."

Terry looked at the surrounding throng. No one said anything. In fact, most of the people seemed to be trying to avoid his eyes, except for the two soldiers, who were looking at him sternly. "Gloria," he said firmly. "Princess Gloria of Medulla. I know her well."

"Ah," said Brimble, nodding sagely. "I see where the trouble lies. No, Sir Knight, you are no longer in Medulla. You crossed the border into Oblongata."

Terry pointed. "That stream is the border. We're on the Medulla side of it."

"Not anymore." One of the soldiers stopped his horse and joined in the conversation.

"That's right," said Brimble. "Who would think that they'd finally settle that border dispute after all these years? But they signed a treaty just a fortnight ago, and the border between Medulla and Oblongata shifted about three miles. Our Village of Dasgut changed possession. King Dafoe is our regent now, and Princess Jane is his only daughter. And your bride-to-be, of course."

Terry looked at him with horror. "Princess Jane Dafoe of Oblongata? *Crazy Jane* Dafoe?"

Brimble sucked his breath in sharply. He looked nervously up at the soldier, then back at Terry. "Really, Sir Knight, crazy is a most ungallant term. It's hardly fair to apply it to a simple, warm-hearted girl like the Princess Jane. One might simply say that she marches to the beat of a different drummer."

The townspeople around them nodded, and Terry heard low murmurs of agreement. "Not crazy, really."

"Eccentric, more like."

"Unconventional."

"Perhaps a bit quirky."

"Totally batshit," said the soldier, resting his hand on his sword.

"She talks to animals!" said Terry.

"And why should anyone have a problem with that?" said Brimble. "It's not uncommon for girls to murmur words of endearment to their little puppies and kittens. It's rather charming, in fact. And who's to say that there's no point to it? I myself had a hound dog like that. A wonderful dog, and very intelligent. He'd look at you and thump his tail, and you would swear he understood every word you said."

"To dead animals!"

"The ability to commune with spirits should not be gainsaid," counseled Brimble. "Can you deny that there are some among us whose senses seem to extend beyond our own, who hold powers that cannot be explained by natural philosophy? Does an afterlife exist for beasts as well as humans? Consider that when our animal companions have crossed the void into that nether world, their voices may indeed . . ."

"Dead cooked animals! Long, involved conversations with pot roasts!"

"Let me explain something," said the mounted soldier. He was trying to keep a friendly tone, but he wasn't trying very hard. The way he leaned over Terry, and the way the other soldier pressed in, carried an undeniable air of menace. "When you perform a service to the kingdom, like you just did, and the king offers his daughter's hand in marriage, it's not just a tradition. It's a point of honor, right? You don't marry his daughter, it's like you're disrespecting her. Which is not a good thing. Because if you disrespect his daughter, it's like you're disrespecting the king. It's an insult."

"And you don't want to insult our king," said the second soldier.

"That's right, you don't. So you're going to see King Dafoe and claim your reward, understand? Nice and respectful, like. And to make sure you don't get lost and accidentally wander off somewhere, we're going to escort you to him."

"Because he's been trying to marry off his loony daughter for years," said the second soldier.

"Shut up," said the first soldier. "Now, my personal advice to you is that when you meet the king, you show that you're real happy about his generous offer of matrimony. Then he won't be ordering us to defend his honor."

"Me?" said Terry with surprise. "Meet the . . . ah, I see the cause of the misunderstanding. You think *I* slew the dragon. Not at all, not at all. Pardon me for not making myself clear. When I said I slew the dragon, of course I was speaking not for myself, but on behalf of my master, the brave Sir Huggins." He threw out his arms and gestured expansively across the meadow, where Huggins was approaching, with the mallet and horse spike in his hands.

"Him?" said Brimble, in a tone of voice that people often used when talking about Huggins.

"The bravest and most gallant knight ever to grace the Twenty Kingdoms. There is no other knight that can compare with him. Please don't let his appearance fool you. He likes to adopt a common manner and dress, so as to humble himself. When you're as skilled as Sir Huggins, it's too easy to become prideful, he tells me. Just treat him as you would anyone else. He prefers it."

"But you're wearing armor," said the first soldier.

"It belongs to Sir Huggins. He bade me put it on. He's very thoughtful that way. 'Terry,' he said to me, 'I slay dragons like other men swat flies, but this one may be dangerous to you, my faithful squire. Take my armor and put it on, that you may be protected. I shall fight the beast without it. Virtue, and the grace of the King, are all the armor I need.' I tell you, tears came to my eyes when he spoke to me thus."

"Sure," said the soldier doubtfully. He tugged on his reins and walked his horse over to Huggins, who was just then coming into earshot. "You, sir," he demanded. "Did you kill that beast?"

Huggins had unslung his pack and put the mallet and spike away. Now he looked at his hands. "Had to," he said regretfully. "They're no good to anyone in that condition. It's a tough job, but really the only thing you can do is put them down."

The crowd nodded. The soldier was not convinced. "You put your steel through its head? You and you alone? You swear this?"

"Oh yes." Huggins patted his pockets, searching for his flask. "Best way to do it. A quick blow, right in the forehead. They hardly feel it. You don't want them to suffer, do you?" He uncorked his flask, which turned out to be empty. He gave it a look of reproach.

"Um, I suppose not," said the soldier, who had never really concerned himself with a dragon's feelings.

"You have to be merciful, you know. They're just

dumb animals. They don't understand why sometimes we have to kill them."

"I guess you're right. Well, sir." The soldier made up his mind. "Let me congratulate you." He bowed from his horse.

"Huh? What for? I just did what had to be done."

"He *is* modest," Brimble confirmed to his people. They murmured their assent. Raising his voice, and striding over to Huggins, he said, "And let me, sir, be the first to buy you a drink."

"Why do—a drink, did you say? Why yes, thank you. I could go with a cool one about now."

"And I'll buy the next one," said the soldier.

"Thank you."

"The first of many rounds, I'm sure," said Brimble. He threw an arm around Huggins' shoulders. "Come on back to my inn, sir, and keep your money in your pocket, for the people of Dasgut will wine you and feast you. Tonight we celebrate!"

"That's very generous of you," said Huggins. He looked around for Terry, who had quietly disappeared. "A celebration, eh? Well, you can tell me about it over a pint."

A long time ago, when the world was yet unex-plored, and every voyage was an adventure, even the most knowledgeable cartographers would write on the edge of their maps the foreboding words, "Here be Dragons." Sometimes they drew little pictures to go with it. These words and icons marked the boundary of the known world. From beyond these borders were returned only hints of information, in ships' logs, in explorers' journals, in the legends and songs of mysterious natives. Except in the case of the Twenty Kingdoms, that cluster of fairy-tale countries that lay in a broad band between the mountains and the sea. Their cartographers also wrote, "Here be Dragons" at the edge of their maps, but they were likely to put it in the center as well. And at the bottom. Or the top, and the sides. Wherever it was needed, because the wretched beasts had a nasty way of poking up where they were least wanted. Which was pretty much anywhere.

It produced a certain amount of tension between the cartographers and the town fathers. The town fathers thought it was bad for business to be associated with dragons. When a new map was about to be released they would send a letter to the cartographer. They would point out that their village had excellent restaurants, that the local brews were superb, that the taxes were kept reasonably low, and the streets were kept clean. They would say that the nearby forest was lush and green, and the surrounding farmland was rich and fertile. They would mention the fresh air and the friendly people. They would vehemently deny that the brand-new performing arts center, designed and built by an award-winning architectural firm, was sinking at a rate of four inches per year. All in all, they would say, their village was a wonderful place to raise a family or start a new business, and taking into consideration its many superior qualities, surely it was only fair to disregard that teensy bit of unpleasantness with the dragon?

The cartographer would not be persuaded. He would set aside his reference books, take up his quill, and eventually send back a polite, noncommittal letter saying that all sources of information had been carefully checked, and perhaps enclose a coupon for 40 percent off the new edition. Then he would publish his map exactly as he intended. Usually that was the end of the matter. Sometimes the debate grew acrimonious. Sometimes letters would fly back and forth, lawsuits would be threatened, and the cartographer would have to play his trump card. He would hint darkly that if he chose to do so, he could mention things that were worse than dragons.

Invariably that was enough to make his critics shut up. For everyone knew that while the Twenty Kingdoms were lands of magic and enchantment, of gallant knights and lovely ladies, of stone and moss and oak and crystal and wild, fierce, beautiful vistas, they did indeed contain some things that were much worse than dragons.

Even under the best of conditions, the city of Sulcus was not a pleasant place to live. In the summer it was hot and damp, and in the winter it was cold and damp. It was a good place from which to govern, because it was located nearly in the center of Medulla, but people who were not connected with the palace tended to move to Occipital on the coast, which had nice beaches and a better climate. Occipital, being a port city, also had better night life. Most Sulcuns did not agree with this. They pointed out that Sulcus had the museums, the monuments, the university, the library, and in general was a center of learning and culture. Sulcuns generally thought of Occipitans as frivolous beachcombing deadbeats. Occipitans replied that Sulcuns were boring stick-in-the-muds who didn't know how to party.

Sulcuns tended to take this personally.

It was a chilly, wet, overcast autumn day all across Medulla, the air heavy with moisture that was too thick for mist and not quite heavy enough for rain. In Sulcus the wind blew the smoke from the chimneys down into the streets, where it added to the murk and mist. In the center of the city the white stone walls of Medulla Palace rose like chalk cliffs above a foggy lake. It was not a day for waiting outside. The streets were muddy, the shop windows were gray with condensation, and in the barren branches the birds fluffed their feathers and eyed Mina with disapproval. The girl was standing beneath a tree, at the edge of a small square near the center of the city. She was the smallest and youngest of the palace maids. She had a coin in her hands and was desperately afraid of losing it. She had knotted it into a piece of cloth, but did not dare put it into her apron pocket, too afraid that the next time she reached for it, it wouldn't be there. It was her first time out of the palace since she had come to the city. She longed to go into one of the shops, but she couldn't take the risk that someone might recognize her. Nor could she stand in the street, for fear of being seen from one of the palace windows. So she twisted the coin in her hands and stood with her back to the tree and peered around the corner.

Most of the people who walked past ignored her, huddled into their cloaks and coats, intent on their own business. But several times men slowed down to look Mina over. Nervously, she kept her eyes on the ground and tried not to notice them. Suddenly she became aware of a man standing next to her, staring down at her. He had a crooked mouth and eyes that squinted, and a bundle of coarsely printed booklets under his arm, wrapped in an oilskin. Involuntarily she took a step backward, coming up against the tree trunk. Water dripped on them both. He made an impatient sound, "Tchah." Then, without a another word, he plucked the piece of cloth from Mina's hand, shoved one of the booklets at her, and walked off down the street with long strides.

Mina shoved the booklet under her apron and ran the four blocks back to the palace. She slipped in the kitchen door, grateful that the task was finished, glad to be out of the damp cold, and into the damp warmth of the kitchen, surrounded by smells of cooked meats and the bustle of kitchen maids. Junie, the oldest maid, said, "You're late."

"The man was late," Mina said meekly.

"She's not late," said Trixie, who was from Mina's own town and her best friend in Sulcus. "Did you get it, Mina? No, don't show it here. Take it upstairs."

"Brush her hair first," said Junie to Trixie. "This is an important meeting. We're having visitors."

"What!" Trixie was alarmed. She looked to see that the door was closed and took Junie's arm. "We can't have visitors! Who else knows about this?"

"Shush, it's okay." The other maids were staring. "They're from the very top," Junie said. "We can trust them."

"Who are they? Tell me!"

"Keep your voice down. You'll know who they are, but don't say their names. Now take Mina upstairs. If we dawdle too long, we'll lose the light. I'll be right up."

The girls swallowed their curiosity. They exchanged their aprons for fresh, clean ones, and went up the back stairs, up five floors to the highest level of the castle, to a small garret with a window that gathered in a few rays from the struggling sun. There were no chairs or other furniture in the room, merely a few storage trunks, but the girls had stocked it with cushions so they could sit in a circle on the floor. Mina was breathless. It was the first time the older girls had let her in on their secret meeting, and she felt very proud to have earned their trust. There were ten girls here already, five from the kitchen, three upstairs maids, one of the parlormaids, and the gardener's girl. Balls of wool and spools of thread lay in their laps, and their nimble fingers automatically manipulated knitting needles, darning needles, tatting needles, sewing needles, and crochet hooks. Trixie shot the bolt on the door. Mina gave the booklet to Trixie, who passed it to the parlormaid, who put it in her knitting bag, and arranged herself so that the light from the window came over her shoulder. Trixie and Mina took their seats on the floor, and for a moment the room filled with the rustle of skirts as the circle spread out to make room for them. They waited, looking at the door, until there was a quiet knock.

Trixie got up and unbolted the door. Junie slipped in, followed by four more girls. Two of the newcomers were wearing dark cloaks of linsey-woolsey, with the hoods pulled over their heads, concealing their faces in shadow. Still, everyone knew who they were, particularly since they had their personal maids with them. The circle spread out again to give everyone extra room. The two princesses reached under their cloaks and produced tatting needles, for even those of royal blood were taught that a girl's hands should never be idle. When they were all settled the older of the two, the princess whose blond hair was peeping out from under her hood, said, "Rowena, you may begin."

The parlormaid folded back the cover and began to read. *"Passion's Chains—or—The White Slavers of Alhambra.* Chapter Nineteen.

Racksturm handed her a quill without meeting her eyes. "You will write them a note," he said harshly. "You must make them understand what will happen to you if they do not pay the ransom."

"My family cannot pay it," she cried desperately. "It will impoverish them!"

He stared out the window, his broad, muscular shoulders silhouetted against the setting sun. "They can sell their land."

Melanie gasped. Sell Eventide? Sell the only place that she could call home, the only place where she had ever been happy. It was unthinkable! She would never ask her grandfather to do such a thing. Defiantly, she flung the quill on the table. "You may do your worst to me, Sir Racksturm, but I will not submit to your demands."

He whirled and seized her arms in his powerful hands. Once again she found herself unable to offer resistance, overwhelmed by his sheer strength and will. "You little fool! Can't you understand? I need that money, for reasons I cannot yet explain."

His callousness stabbed her heart like a sword, but she held his gaze. "Is that all you care about, the money? Does nothing else have meaning for you, even after . . ." She nearly choked on the words. "After everything that has happened?"

"Damn you!" Racksturm swore, and then he had her in his arms, taking her kiss, covering her mouth with his and crushing their lips together. His fingers found her bodice and ripped the laces free of the satin cloth, leaving her tender flesh to his mercy. She did not protest, arching her back like a young willow blown by a savage storm, and forcing her breasts against him. Racksturm held her tighter and tighter still, but she felt no pain, only the growing heat within her own body, and the passionate swelling of his . . . oh!"

Rowena dropped the booklet. "I can't breathe." Her face was flushed and her breath came in short pants.

"Loosen her stays," the Princess Gloria commanded. "Open that window." She stood up and took Rowena by the arm, supporting her in front of the window until the thoroughly embarrassed maid regained her composure. Cool air blew across them both. "Feel better now?" The girl nodded. "Want to stay for the rest of it?" Another nod. "Perhaps someone else will read for a while. Junie?"

Junie collected the booklet, and the circle settled back down. The clicking of needles resumed. But before she could read a word, there was yet another knock on the door. The group gave a collective sigh of exasperation. "Now what?" said Gloria.

Her maid unbolted the door. A small boy, dressed in blue serge and brass buttons, stood at attention. "Beg pardon, Miss Alice, but Her Royal Majesty the Queen of Medulla requires the presence of the Princess Gloria immediately." He looked in the door. "Hi, Mina."

"All right, Sammy," Alice told the page. "You may tell

the Queen that I know where the Princess is and will convey the message immediately." She was not surprised that the page had found their "secret" meeting. Somehow the small boys seemed to know every nook and cubbyhole in the palace. Which was, no doubt, why they were used as pages. She reached out to pat him on the head, but the boy ducked away and took off. The maid closed the door firmly.

The Princess Jennifer sprang to her feet. "Yes! It's your engagement! She's going to announce your engagement." She took Gloria's hands and pulled her up. "That's got to be it."

"We shall see," said Gloria calmly. She let herself out the door. Alice started to follow, but Gloria sent her back inside. "Please, don't let me interrupt. Go ahead and finish." She walked to the staircase, with Jennifer on her heels, then turned around in time to see the rest of the girls streaming through the door. Having dutifully waited an entire ten seconds, they now spread out to carry the news to the castle.

Gloria kept her own excitement in check until she reached her dressing room, where she discarded her cloak and let her afternoon gown fall to the floor. Slipping into a champagne-colored silk sheath, she found her hands shaking too much to fasten the buttons. Jennifer helped her with them. "I wish I could wear my new rose gown with the lace blouse. But I've earmarked it for the Autumn Ball."

"I'm having a black lace dress made for the ball. But my seamstress says there may not be enough lace for it."

"Every year the dressmakers say that, but every year there's always enough lace. Don't worry about it." The princess held a gold ring against her ear, looked at herself in the mirror, and discarded it for another pair.

"Who do you think it is? There have been so many of them."

"It's Terry, of course." Gloria was certain of this.

Jennifer was not. "It's not Terry, Gloria. Don't get your hopes up. He only has a knighthood. He's not of the nobility."

"A knight can be introduced in court. That's all Mother needs to be concerned about."

"He has no money. Mother would never betroth you to a landless knight."

Gloria settled on earrings and fastened them on. "My Terry is not a landless knight. He has property in Middleton. It brings him fifty royals a year."

"Fifty royals a year is not much. My Georgy has nine hundred royals a year, and the largest private estate in Medulla."

"You young girls think too much of money," said Gloria, who was nineteen. She gave her hair a few extra strokes with a silver hairbrush. "Money is not important. What's important is that a man be strong and brave and daring. But he must also be loyal and kindhearted. And good-looking, of course. As long as a man has these noble qualities, and fifty royals a year, then a girl should be happy with him. Do I need more powder?"

"No, you're fine. You won't get any money from Mother and Father if you marry Terry. You know that. What will you live on? You can't live on fifty royals a year."

"You certainly can, if you manage your money carefully. Fifty royals a year will get us a house in Middleton with a cook, a maid-of-all-work, and, of course, Terry's squire. We can also afford a gardener to come in once a week, or perhaps an upstairs maid. I haven't decided yet."

"You can't keep a stable on fifty a year. You won't have a carriage. My Georgy has two matched teams of carriage horses, in addition to his riding horses."

"We won't need a carriage. Middleton is on the coach line. My Terry keeps his horse at the livery stable, and we can rent a carriage when we come into the city. Should I put up my hair?"

"Yes," said Jennifer firmly. "This is a formal announcement."

"Bring me those pins, will you, please?"

Her sister rummaged around the dressing table and returned with hairpins. "What about schools? You won't be able to send your children away to school."

"Middleton happens to have an excellent day school," said Gloria smugly.

"You've thought of everything, haven't you?"

"We'll be able to afford two weeks at the seashore each summer and give two dinner parties each season. I've added it all up."

"You'll be bored," said Jennifer darkly. "Bored, bored, bored. You won't like it in the country. You'll be coming to the city every week to visit my Georgy and me."

"Fresh milk!" returned Gloria. "Fresh eggs. You and Georgy will be coming to the country each week to dine with us." She gave her hair a final pat. "Let's go. Where are my gloves?"

Jennifer followed Gloria to the grand staircase but hung back at the top of the stairs. Since this was Gloria's moment, it was appropriate that no one else should divert attention from her when she made her big entrance. And a big entrance it was. The grand stairway descended to a marbled hall that rose three stories. Highly polished parquet floors waited to greet her. Candles glittered in every nook and cranny, and reflected off the giant cut-glass chandelier that dominated the ceiling. Portraits of Medulla's former kings, queens, and major lottery winners hung on the walls. Gloria could almost imagine that they were smiling at her, congratulating her, giving their approval to the match. The princess descended the stairs slowly, one hand caressing the walnut banister, her silk dress trailing behind her, hair piled on top of her head, a calm smile on her lovely face, bright blue eyes serenely confident. Word had spread quickly through the palace. It seemed as though every one of the royal family's personal servants had somehow contrived to be doing something in the big hallway when Gloria came down. She nodded to each one as she passed them by and entered the antechamber to the queen's drawing room. It was crowded to near bursting, filled with courtiers, nobles, politicians, the ladies who formed the queen's inner circle, and, of course, the lawyers who negotiated the betrothal. They all bowed as she passed. A footman opened the door to the queen's drawing room. She went inside and stood still until she heard the door close behind her.

The queen was exuberantly happy. She was dressed in a severe dark jacket and skirt, with little makeup, for she had been taking part in the negotiations herself and trying to look tough. Now that they were over she floated around the room giving directions to the waiters, who were setting out champagne flutes and trays of petits fours. One bottle was already open. Between instructions the queen danced around the room with a glass in each hand and hummed a little children's song. When Gloria came in, her mother rushed over to kiss her on the cheek, then handed her a glass of champagne. "Gloria, dear, I am so, so happy for you!"

"Yes, Mother."

"You will be so, so pleased with man we have for you."

"I'm sure I will, Mother," said Gloria, thinking of Terry.

"Come here and sit with me." The queen took Gloria's hand and pulled her over to a couch. Gloria sat on the edge of her seat, while the queen settled back among the cushions. "Well, dear, we've all been working very hard for this, but I'm sure you'll agree that he is worth the wait."

"I'm sure I will, Mother."

"He is virtuous and educated and intelligent."

"Oh yes."

"Oh, Gloria!" Here the queen clutched her daughter's arm. "He is so handsome. Oh, wait until you see him. You will not be able to take your eyes off him."

"No," breathed Gloria.

"There has never been a match like this. You will be the envy of every girl in the kingdom. I just know you'll be perfect together."

"I know," said Gloria, smiling.

The queen beamed at her. "Well, I won't keep you in suspense any longer. As of today, you are officially engaged to . . ." The queen paused dramatically. "Roland Westfield."

"Um," said Gloria. Her brain suddenly seemed to slow down. It was as if all her thoughts were mired in taffy and had to be extracted one by one. She saw her mother looking at her expectantly, waiting for a reaction, and she tried to think of something to say, but all that she could manage was a second, "Um."

The queen patted her arm, cheerfully sympathetic. "I know how you feel, dear. You wait and wait for the news, but when it actually happens it all seems so unexpected and overwhelming."

"Unexpected," said Gloria, looking vaguely around the room. "Yes." She felt dizzy. Her eyes settled on the glass in her hand. She stared at it until she was able to focus again, took a tiny sip, then tossed back the rest in a gulp. "Roland Westfield. I know of him, I think. Wait. Westfield? Not the Westfield Bakeries Westfields?"

"Yes," said her mother, a bit smugly. "They are very, very rich."

"They certainly are," said Gloria sharply. "Very rich indeed! And you know how they get their money, don't you?"

"Of course, dear. They hold the patents on sliced bread."

"Exactly!" Gloria stood up. "Mother, how could you do this?"

"Now, Gloria, don't get started on the sliced bread issue. There's nothing wrong with eating sliced bread. It's perfectly safe."

"You don't know that! No one can be sure of that!" Gloria's emotions began to heat up. "Sliced bread has never been adequately tested. We don't know what the long-term health effects are!"

The queen dismissed this. "When you are married to Roland you can influence him to change his policies."

She fluttered her hand. "Or whatever you like. Now, let's go out and make the announcement. We mustn't keep the guests waiting."

Gloria clutched her empty glass. "A moment, Mother. When was the betrothal agreement signed?"

The queen looked surprised. "Not an hour ago, dear. Why do you ask? I sent for you as soon as I could."

"Yes. I appreciate that, Mother. But wasn't there news—this morning? I mean, the news came this morning, but it must have happened days ago. About a dragon? And a knight? I know I heard something about this. You know, that big dragon in the south? Father has been trying for years to get someone to slay it."

"Why yes, dear. There was a dragon slain down that way. Was that bothering you? We know all about it." The Queen patted Gloria on the shoulder. "But you have nothing to worry about. It won't affect our plans at all. The knight who slew it chased it over the border into Oblongata."

"He what!"

"And now he's going to marry Princess Jane."

"Jane!"

"I'm so happy for her. She's waited so long for this, poor dear. I mean, she's such . . ." Now it was the queen's turn to study her glass while she combed her mind for the right word. "Such an *unusual* girl. A lovely person really, in her own way. I suppose we'll be invited to the wedding. That will be nice. It's been such a long time since we've seen them."

"Let's hope she doesn't get in an argument with the pork chops again," said Gloria, still mentally reeling from the news.

"Curiously, it turned out to be one of our own knights who did the slaying, although I'm not familiar with his name. I think you made a fortunate escape, Gloria. From what I've been told, he seems to be a coarse and vulgar sort of fellow."

"He certainly is not! I happen to know he's a very fine young man."

"I'm glad to hear it. Well, I think we've kept them waiting long enough. Are you ready?" Without waiting for an answer, she led Gloria into the antechamber. A line of waiters followed with trays, cutting off escape. Immediately they were surrounded by courtiers. Gloria accepted the bows and curtseys and congratulations with an absentminded smile. But while she made light conversation, her eyes flicked around the room. It took a while to find the man she was seeking, because he in turn was trying to avoid her gaze, but eventually she cornered him. "Counselor Miligras," she said, beaming at him. "It is so good to see you again."

"Thank you, Princess," said the lawyer, trying to discreetly edge away, but finding his path blocked by others.

"I do so appreciate the work you put into this. I know it has been a long and difficult negotiation."

Miligras wore a high, stiff collar, which seemed to be getting higher and stiffer as he shrank down into it. He ran a finger around his neck. "I can't take all the credit, Your Highness. There were others involved. I was part of a team." His voice held a bit of a plea. "It wasn't only me."

"I hope both you and your coworkers will accept my thanks for your efforts. But Counselor Miligras," she continued, "it's all so complicated and confusing to a simple girl like myself. I wonder if I could speak privately to you about it? Just to clear up a few issues?"

"Of course, of course. That's what I'm here for. Always happy to be of service, Your Highness. I think I have an opening in my schedule next Tuesday . . ."

"Right now, please, if you would be so kind," said Gloria sweetly. "There's an empty room next door. Really, I won't take but a minute of your time."

She gestured toward a connecting door. Miligras courteously opened it for her and followed her in. It was merely a small waiting room where the queen's ladies-in-waiting could write a few letters or play cards while waiting to attend on Her Royal Majesty. (Ladies-in-waiting do a lot of waiting.) Gloria smiled patiently, hands clasped in front of her as Miligras closed the door behind them and turned the key in the lock. When he was certain it was secure he straightened his back, adjusted his cravat, turned to face Gloria, and said authoritatively, "Now, Princess, I understand you have every reason to be upset . . ."

Two small but strong hands grabbed his collar, dragged him to a chair, and pushed him down in it so hard it rocked back on two legs. He flung his arms out to keep from toppling over. "Miligras," yelled Gloria. "What the hell do you think you're doing! I paid you a huge chunk of my allowance this year! You're supposed to stomp down every other suitor, and now this? You got me engaged to some pretty boy!"

The attorney shrank back in his chair. "It was unavoidable, Princess. The family is wealthy, and the pressure was so great—I warned you I couldn't hold them off forever—but you know I've done my best for you all these months—and then the news came in this morning that Sir Terry would marry Princess Jane—and all the women on the team were so gaga over this Roland lad—so I thought, *well, at least that will be some consolation to her.* Because they all think he's so good-looking. So I withdrew my objections, and we went ahead with it."

"My Terry is not going to marry Jane," Gloria said definitely.

"But Your Highness, it's a done deal. I'm sorry, Princess, but you can't interfere with another country's nuptial arrangements. I mean yes, it can be done. The King can do it, Medulla as a country can do it, countries do it all the time, but it's a diplomatic issue. You personally can't do anything. If I start poking my nose over there and making queries, people will figure out that you're behind it. Your parents certainly will. Besides, even if Sir Terry managed to break his engagement to Princess Jane, it would be an intolerable scandal. A woman of your position couldn't possibly marry him afterward. As for your own engagement, the Westfields are very influential. They really want this marriage. And they've got a damn good negotiating team."

"Stall them," said Gloria curtly. She walked around the chair as she spoke, thinking hard. Miligras had to crane his neck to keep her in sight. "Don't break the engagement, just delay things. Say there are still a few details to work out. It doesn't matter if the contract has been signed. You told me a good lawyer can examine a receipt for a coffee and a bun and find loopholes in it. You can hold this up."

Miligras had heard mention of certain female insects that, for one reason or another, would bite the heads off male insects that displeased them. The Princess Gloria, he thought, seemed to have the same frame of mind. He cleared his throat nervously and said, "Ah, I suppose there are a few details to . . ."

"Fine," said Gloria. "Take care of it. And I'll need some of your couriers. Not the royal couriers, but the private, confidential couriers that you use for legal business." She stopped in front of him and jerked her head toward the door. "Give me an hour to finish up in there. Then send one of them to my rooms."

"Oh my God," said Miligras. "This isn't another one of your plans, is it?"

"Just do it," Gloria said.

As a man with an earned knighthood, Terry was required to put in his months of annual service to the king. Because he chose to serve in the Royal Guard, he was generally able to enter the palace without anyone taking much notice. The night of his return was a little bit different. It was a clandestine meeting, so he was not in uniform. He cleaned up and changed clothes as soon as he arrived back at the city; but he was stiff and sore from the fracas with the dragon, and he still looked as if he had been in a fight. Nonetheless, he was able to avoid the guards on duty, let himself in through a little-used service entrance, and make his way to a suite of offices used by scriveners during the day and by no one at night. The Princess was already there, waiting for him. Gloria had concealed herself again in a loose cloak and hood, but Terry was able to recognize her immediately. This was because she launched herself at him the moment she saw him and covered his face with kisses.

When they eventually disentangled, Gloria explained

about Roland, and Terry explained about Jane. The whole story took a bit of time, because he periodically had to wait for Gloria to stop giggling. "Huggins?" she said. "Omigod, Huggins! Oh, the poor, poor man." She started laughing again.

"It's not funny," said Terry, although it was, and he had to work to hide his own smile. "I still owe him for this month's wages. I'll have to send a cheque."

"We must send a wedding present. What shall it be? For Huggins, something he can drink, I suppose."

"I'm sure he'll appreciate anything that comes in a cask."

Gloria grabbed Terry's hand. She tugged him into an empty room, found a tinderbox on a table by the door, and passed it to Terry. "I have a surprise for you. Light that candle over there, please."

Terry lit a candle while Gloria lit a lamp. Light suffused the small office. Gloria stood in the middle of the room, holding her cloak tight around herself, the hood pulled close to her face. He waited expectantly. When she was sure she had his attention, she flung off the cloak with a dramatic flourish, and did a little pirouette. "What do you think?"

"About what?"

"Do you notice anything different about me?"

Long experience had taught Terry the answer to this question. "You've lost weight!" he said approvingly. "And you look great! Of course you looked great before, but now the extra definition really enhances your . . ."

"Wrong," snapped Gloria. "Try again."

"A new dress," said Terry enthusiastically. "It looks great! The color goes so well with your eyes."

"Are you blind? Sometimes I swear all men are blind."
She tossed her head and pointed at her hair. "I changed
my hair color."

Terry carefully looked her over. "No you didn't."

"Of course I did. It's blond."

"It was blond."

"Not this blond. Before it was Light Honey Gold, and
now it's Medium Almond Sunburst."

"It looks the same."

Gloria crossed her arms. "I don't believe this. You
know, Terry, women go through a lot of trouble to look
good for their men, and the least you men can do is try to
show some appreciation."

"I get my hair cut every month. I don't jump in front
of every woman I meet and say, 'Well, what do you
think?' "

"That's because your hair always looks the same."

But yours does look the same, Terry knew enough not
to say. Instead, he chose a strategic retreat. He took her
arm and gently guided her closer to the lamp. "Well, of
course," he said with conviction. "The light wasn't good
enough for me to tell at first, but now that you're nearer
the lamp I can see the dramatic difference. Yes, it's beautiful. It is truly quite striking."

"Do you really think so?" said Gloria, cuddling closer
to him.

Terry stroked her hair. "Of course. It looks great. And
the color goes so well with your eyes."

"Such a charmer," murmured Gloria. She gave him a
finishing kiss, then got businesslike. "Now then. If anyone asks, you've been hunting at Lord George's lodge for
the past month. I'll tell Jenny to tell George to support

your story. No one keeps track—there are always hunting parties going on there for boar and hart. Tomorrow I'll go to the College of Heraldry. I know a few of the clerks there. It won't cost much to have them cobble up a coat of arms for Huggins and slip it into the records. Did anyone see your crest?"

"It's on my armor."

"The *preux chevalier*, right? A helm with a red mantle? I'll have the clerk develop something that looks similar for Huggins. Probably no one in Dasgut will remember your crest, but if the question does come up, they'll just think they were confused."

"Good."

"I'll also visit the records clerk at the tournament committee and have him insert Sir Huggins into the lists for a few past tourneys. As long as we don't pretend he actually won a contest, no one will make an issue of it." Gloria thought for a minute. "That ought to provide enough back-story for a quick check. I doubt anyone will look at Huggins' past history very closely. People over here won't care. People over there—well—King Dafoe is really eager to get Jane married off."

"Huggins will adapt," said Terry. "Life's a stage, we all have our parts to play, and the role of a gentleman of leisure just suits him. Although . . ." He looked pensive.

"What's wrong, sweetie?"

"Ah, well, it's just that . . . I don't know." Terry looked away, suddenly embarrassed that he was displaying too much emotion. "I mean, how many knights ever manage to slay a dragon? How many knights have ever even seen a dragon? And now that I've done it, I have to give the credit to someone else. My squire gets to be a hero. Of course," he continued swiftly, afraid his mood might be misinterpreted, "it's worth it for you, honey. But if you have to marry Roland anyway . . ."

"You're a hero to me, Terry."

"Aw, Gloria. You're so sweet. That makes me feel totally pathetic."

"I'm sorry." Gloria hugged him. "I know you really slew the dragon, sweetie. It was very noble of you to give up the credit. And we *are* getting married. Don't worry about Roland. I have a plan."

She cast about for her cloak. Terry helped her arrange it over her shoulders. "Whatever you have is bound to turn out better than my dragon-slaying plan. What is it?"

The Princess patted his hand. "I'll tell you when the time is right. We'll get married, and you'll be a hero, too. Now you go off and report for duty tomorrow as though you were returning from a hunting trip. Wait for a message from me. And don't worry about Roland."

Roland tried to look conservative. He had left his elegant silk shirts in the closet, choosing instead a more conventional shirt of ordinary white linen. He ignored his trendy brocaded jackets in favor of plain gray homespun. He left off all his jewelry and wore the same simple belt buckle and black boots that his father and uncles favored. He had even considered cutting his long hair, but eventually decided just to get it trimmed and tie it in a ponytail, which he then tucked under the back of his collar. He did his best to make a good impression, that of a serious, mature businessman, and now, sitting at the long conference table with his relatives, he realized that he had failed utterly.

"Caraway seeds," his Aunt Agatha was saying. She was the oldest of the dozen Westfield family members seated around the long conference table, three years older than her husband, and although everyone pretended not to know that, she led every meeting. Her voice was absolutely flat and expressionless, carrying no hint of the disdain that Roland knew she was feeling, the same disdain she showed for all his ideas. Of course, she had never actually flat-out rejected any of his ideas. She would say something like, "We find your ideas interesting," or "We'll consider your proposal carefully," or sometimes just "I see." This was going the same way.

"Seeded rye bread," said Roland brightly. He was trying to keep a positive tone, hoping the enthusiasm would be contagious, but a note of desperation was starting to creep into his voice. "The richness of rye bread blended with a subtle hint of caraway . . ."

"Do people eat a lot of caraway seed, Roland?"

"Not per se, no. But research shows that when mixed with rye dough . . ."

"You seem to be doing a lot of research with seeds, Roland." His Uncle Jeffrey flipped through a stack of old proposals that he had brought with him. All of them had been written by Roland, all had been rejected at previous meetings. "Poppy seeds on hard rolls, sesame seeds on buns, lemon muffins with . . ." He scanned the proposal. "Poppy seeds again."

"All those products did very well in the test markets," said Roland. "As did these." He had prepared sample loaves of bread, which were now sitting in covered baskets in the center of the conference table. None of the committee members had bothered to touch them.

"And now rye bread with caraway seeds," said Aunt Agatha. She poked at a basket, pushing it down the table, away from her. "Is there perhaps some reason for this obsession with seeds, Roland?"

"The reason is sales," said Roland. "Sales of sliced bread have been flat . . ." It was the wrong thing to say. Expressions hardened all around the table. His family was not prepared to face bad news. He tried to recover. "I'm just saying that the movement toward natural foods is growing. We need to give the health food people a product they can get behind. Seeds, nuts, berries, they love that stuff. By adding seeds to our products we can . . ."

"I see," said Aunt Agatha.

"Roland," interrupted his Uncle Stimson. "I hate to belabor the ludicrously obvious, but bread is made from seeds. That's what flour is, finely ground seeds of wheat and rye. It doesn't need more seeds."

"Although we do find your ideas interesting," said Aunt Agatha.

"Don't be discouraged, Roland," said Uncle Jeffrey. "You may rest assured that we'll consider your proposal carefully. Now, to the next item of business."

And that was it. The conversation turned to pricing structures and the cost of flour. Roland collected his papers and departed the conference room. He left the baskets behind. His father excused himself from the group and followed him. At the end of the hallway he caught up with his son and put an arm around his shoulder. "Roland," he said. "I want to tell you again how much

I appreciate your efforts. We all appreciate your efforts."

"They don't appreciate my efforts, Dad. They don't even listen."

"It's a complicated business, son. They've been at it all their lives. It takes time to earn their confidence."

We don't have time, Roland thought. *Not the way the sales of sliced bread are falling. We'll be bankrupt in two years if this keeps on.* He didn't bother to say this. He had said it too many times already.

His father seemed to read his thoughts. "I know, Roland. Sales will recover. We've been through downturns before. Truthfully, the best thing you can do for the family right now is to go ahead with this marriage. A connection to the royal family will help business more than you can imagine. We've worked very hard on this, Roland, for a very long time. We're counting on you to do your part."

"Do what part? Dad, I'm the groom. All I have to do is show up with a ring and a best man. The bride and her mother do all the work." They left the building. It was still before noon, a cool, clear, crisp day, and traffic was heavy. They stood on the edge of the street, waiting for a space to clear among the wagons and rumbling carts.

"That's not true, Roland," his father said, once they had crossed the street. "Don't underestimate your role in this. The groom has a lot of important responsibilities. He has to—um—buy a ring, for example. And choose a best man. And then he has to—uh—show up. Okay, maybe he doesn't have *a lot* of responsibilities, but they're *important* responsibilities. In fact," his father continued, warming to his theme, "showing up is really the key to the whole marriage ceremony."

"Yes, all right, fine," said Roland. They stopped in front of a Westfield Bakery. It was one that Roland had been given personal charge of. "Ring, best man, show up. Got it. You can count on me, Dad. I won't let the family down."

They exchanged pleasantries, then Roland went up the stairs to his office. Rows of books, covering all aspects of cookery, lined the walls. On one side of the door hung a painting of Agatha Teasdale, who was said to have invented the dumpling. The other side held a portrait of Primus Colazius, the philosopher who first postulated a connection between bacon and eggs. A small stove kept the room warm and held a teakettle. As a gentleman, he was forced to refrain from actually taking part in the baking process—the guilds would have a fit if he tried—but an office over a bakery gave him as much control as he could maintain over his test loaves. Even now, the room was filled with the smell of freshly baked bread. Baskets of loaves—wheat, rye, honey nut oatmeal—awaited his approval. Stacks of carefully handwritten recipes stood on his desk, with notes written in both margins. He picked one up. It was a recipe for rye bread. The previous week he had scrawled across it with a charcoal stick, "a sure winner," then added an exclamation mark and circled it. Now he snarled at the paper, tore it in half, and fed the pieces into the stove. With a sudden fury he grabbed the whole stack and dumped it into the stove, which only had the effect of nearly smothering the fire inside. He grabbed a bell off the bookcase and rang for his valet. "Neville," he said when the man appeared, "you see all this bread?" Roland gestured at the baskets lining the wall.

"Sire?"

"Take it to the almshouse and tell them to give it to the poor."

"Yes, Sire. I will fetch a few of the delivery boys."

"Fine. And Neville?"

"Sire?"

"Man does not live by bread alone."

"No, Sire."

"Go to the market and buy some stuff to go with it. Fruit, cheese, pickles, you know what I mean. Take it all to the almshouse. There's money in the cupboard."

"Yes, Sire."

His valet left, closing the door quietly. A short time later a trio of delivery boys tiptoed in, collected the bread, and tiptoed out again. Roland sat at his desk with his head in his hands, watching the stove, seeing the tiny remaining flames lick at the paper. Before long the fire recovered, eating happily at two years of work. He went through the rest of the paper on his desk. The heavy marriage contract had arrived only a few days ago. He had set it aside to read later. It was wrapped in brown paper, bound with string, and sealed with the royal seal. He cut the string, unwrapped it—and once again set it aside to read later. He went through the latest invoices for the bakery and updated his ledger books. He riffled through a sheaf of marketing studies and added them to the stove. The dancing light did nothing to dispel his gloom. Presently he became aware of a commotion in the street. He went to the window, opened the sash, and looked down. People seemed to be gathering outside. Some seemed to be looking up at him. He frowned and closed the shutters. Before he could return to his chair, the door was flung open by his valet. "Sire!" the man said, a bit breathlessly. "The Princess Gloria has been kidnapped!"

"Really?" Roland sat down, picked up an invoice, and studied it. It was from his glove maker. He would put it into a separate ledger, along with the bills from his hatter and his tailor. "Which one is the Princess Gloria? And why should I care?"

"The oldest one, Sire." His valet pointed to the contract on Roland's desk. "And the one to whom you are engaged."

Roland looked at the first page of the contract and slapped the invoice down on top of it. "Oh, damn it to hell. That's all we need right now."

Galloway IV, King of Medulla, stomped down the second-floor hallway of the east wing of Medulla Palace, a dirty scrap of foolscap scrunched in one hand, the other hand clenched into a fist. The second floor of the east wing was where the royal family had their suites. The floor was carpeted, so stomping didn't have quite the same effect as it did downstairs, but it was still enough to shake the paintings on the walls. The king was a big man. His purple robe, a color reserved for royalty in Medulla, swirled around him as he turned a corner. Underneath his official robes of office he wore flannel pajamas. He had been taking a nap when the news arrived.

Hard on his heels were two of the palace guard—Terry was one of the pair—in thick wool uniforms, with breastplates and cut-and-thrust military swords. For safety's sake they were supposed to precede the king and shelter him from danger, but that was difficult with Galloway, who had a tendency to change directions suddenly and without warning. Terry and the other guards usually found themselves scurrying after the king. Today was no exception.

The guards were followed by a long, strung-out line of worried ministers, courtiers, aides, officers, and assistants. Periodically Galloway turned to them and yelled out things like, "What sort of hoax is this?" and "Bunch of damn nonsense," while waving the paper for emphasis. His sycophants did not comment, and once he turned away, exchanged concerned looks. Terry, who was just as worried as any of the others, tried to conceal his feelings. He had his own note, tightly folded and tucked away in an inner pocket. It did not reassure him.

The King reached a suite of rooms, gave the door three brisk knocks, and entered his daughter's sitting room without listening for a reply. The room was filled with morning sun. An attractive girl was leaning back in the window seat, working on a very difficult cross-stitch. At Galloway's entrance she came to her feet. She was tall, slim, had long blond hair, was primly clothed in a high-necked dress, and she listened respectfully when the king spoke.

He waved the paper under her nose and shouted, "Now see here, Gloria." Upon saying this, he decided that there was no need to shout at the girl, and modulated his voice. "Now see here, Gloria," he repeated in a softer tone. "What's all this folderol about being kidnapped? You've got your mother all upset, and the whole palace is in a tizzy. You know I take a very dim view of these kinds of pranks. Look at you. You're almost a grown woman now. This sort of thing is beneath your dignity."

"I'm sorry, Your Majesty," the girl said politely. "I'm sure you are quite correct. But I regret that I must tell you I'm not your daughter Gloria. I'm Jean, one of her ladies-in-waiting."

"You're not Gloria?"

"No, Your Majesty."

"You're quite sure?"

"Yes, Your Majesty."

"Well, damn it, where is Gloria?"

The rest of the king's entourage was piling up at the door. A small girl in a blue pinafore wiggled her way through the crowd of legs. She ran up to the king and hugged one of his legs. "Hi, Father!"

"You!" The King pointed a finger at her. "Are you Gloria?"

"I'm Melody, Father!"

"All right, then!" The king disentangled himself from the child, pushed forward into the dressing room, and from there into Gloria's bedroom. After a cursory check he returned to the sitting room, which had filled with government officials. More were still outside. "Which one is Gloria, anyway?"

"Gloria is your oldest daughter, Your Majesty," said Jean.

"That's correct, Your Majesty," said Terry.

There were murmurs of assent from both inside the room and those still outside the doorway. A tear welled up in the little girl's eye. "You don't remember me, Father?"

Instantly contrite, the king dropped to his knees and threw an arm around the child. "Of course I remember your name, Melody. I was just checking to see if *you* remembered." He felt in his pocket with his other hand and was gratified to come up with a handful of wrapped peppermints. "Here, have a sweetmeat, *Melody*. Now go and play with your friends, *Melody*." Placated, the girl crunched the candy and ran through the door, the various ministers parting to let her through. "Melody, Melody," the king muttered. He closed his eyes and paced back and forth a bit. "Got to remember . . ." He opened his eyes and saw the courtiers watching him. "What?" he demanded. "You think I don't know my own children? Of course I do . . . you!"

He pointed a finger at another young woman who was poking her head up from behind the crowd in the hall, trying to see what was going on. "You're Gloria! I remember that dress! You posed for a portrait in it. It's hanging in the library. Get in here!"

Once again his entourage separated themselves to form a path for the girl. She slid through them and curtseyed to the king. "I'm sorry, Your Majesty. I'm Alice. I'm Princess Gloria's personal maid."

"It's common for a gentlewoman to make gifts of clothing to her personal maid, Your Majesty," said Jean. "Gloria also makes gifts to her friends."

King Galloway lost his temper. "That's it," he roared. "I've had enough. I want every woman in the castle assembled in the ballroom in one hour! Do you hear me? One hour. In the ballroom." He glared at his assembled ministers. "See to it!"

Precisely one hour later he entered the ballroom, flanked by his guards. He had changed out of his pajamas and combed his hair and beard. His ministers flocked around like nervous birds, crowding up behind him.

Queen Matilda was seated in the center front, openly weeping. The footman had just finished bringing in extra chairs, for the queen had her own entourage, and it was larger than the king's. She was surrounded by children, courtiers, ladies-in-waiting, maids, governesses, cooks, laundresses, dressmakers, tradeswomen, waitresses, teachers, musicians, actresses, artists, friends, and visiting nobility. All looked grave. All stood when the king entered, flanked by his bodyguards. Terry, still on duty, was at the king's side. Galloway strode briskly to the front of the room, held up a hand for silence, and said authoritatively, "Thank you for coming. I know that you are all very busy, but this will take only a moment." He waited for the room to become silent. "I want everyone who is not one of my daughters to sit down. Understood? Everyone who is *not* one of my daughters, please sit down."

There was a rustling of skirts and a sliding of chairs. A hundred feminine eyes watched as the king did a quick head count, then double-checked, his lips moving. He motioned for his chargé d'affaires to come to his side. "I make it out to be nine."

"I get the same total, Your Majesty."

"There should be ten, right?"

"That is correct, Your Majesty."

"Do a roll call. Find out who is . . ."

"It's Princess Gloria, Your Majesty," said Terry quietly.

The king looked at the knight. "You're sure?"

"Yes, Your Majesty."

"He is correct, Your Majesty."

"Well, that jibes with this note, then." He turned to the

watching throng. "All right, then. Dismissed. Thank you for your cooperation." All the women rose, but none left. They were all watching the queen, who remained seated. Galloway cleared his throat nervously, then turned his back on them. He gestured for some of his key ministers to come over. "How could this happen?" he asked in a low voice. He pointed to the note.

"She was riding in the royal park," someone said. "It's always been considered a secure area. She rides there all the time. All your girls do. And since she turned eighteen, Princess Gloria often sends her bodyguards away. She says she needs her privacy. Anyway, the horse came back to the stable without her. The note was pinned to the saddle blanket. It said to wait for instructions."

"I know what it says."

"We combed the park, of course, but we didn't find anything else. There's no reason to think she has been injured. A few witnesses have come forward already. They say a band of brigands rode off to the west. A young blond woman was with them. They said she seemed to be struggling."

"All right then," said the king. "Mobilize the Royal Guard. Start tracking the brigands. Cover all the routes out of the city. Put every available man on it. Round up the usual suspects, offer the usual rewards, you know how it works."

"Yes, Your Majesty."

"Contact me as soon as you learn anything. Wait a minute." King Galloway snapped his fingers. "Gloria. Didn't we finally get her betrothed to that poofy-looking kid?"

"The wealthy young gentleman? Yes, Your Majesty."

"Well, he has a problem, doesn't he?" The King looked over his shoulder, to where the queen was still sitting. She had stopped crying and was now glaring at him. Galloway turned back to his ministers. "Gloria's mother is going to be *so* mad."

The office of the Royal Guard was hot and stuffy. It was located at one end of the palace, near the stables and the barracks, so Terry had to cross both the exercise yard and the stable yard to get to it. A fire burned in the stove, a pot of coffee boiled on top of it, and the Captain of the Guard looked as though he had spent a sleepless night, which he had. He sat at a small conference table, with his elbows on the top and his chin supported by his hands, poring over a large map of the kingdom. He had taken a stick of charcoal and marked the map in a grid pattern. Pins with colored flags and initials represented each knight. Terry looked them over. If the pins were located accurately, the bulk of Medulla's knighthood was spreading out in a wide arc that would cover the western third of the kingdom. The Captain looked up with bleary eyes.

"About time you showed up," was all he said, without taking his head out of his hands.

"I was on duty," said Terry mildly. "I had to wait until His Majesty dismissed me."

"Mmm-mm," said the Captain. He selected a pin, pasted a little triangle of paper to the blunt end, and wrote Terry's initials on the paper with a ragged quill. "The most likely routes have been taken, I'm afraid." He slid the pin over to Terry. "We got everyone off and on their way this morning. Horses, tack, supplies, squires—it took a bit of doing, but they all left at first light. If you want in on this, pick any empty square."

"I need a moment to think about it," said Terry. He poured a cup for himself, and pretended to study the map some more. "You're all pretty certain they went west, eh?"

"Get me some more of that coffee, if you please. Yes, no doubt about it. Three separate witnesses saw her carried off. A young girl, an old woman, and a farm laborer. Rarely do we get such good agreement on stories. Brigands, five of them, with horses, and they went west."

"West makes sense." The western border of Medulla was well-known as bandit country. "Where there's a border, there's smugglers. Where there's travelers, there's bandits."

"Right. Broken terrain, heavy thorn brush, hills, caves, streams, and those damned ravines cutting every which way. You can't ride in a straight line for a mile. That will be a problem. We'll be flushing all sort of thieves and road agents out of there. It just makes it harder to find the ones we actually want."

"I've got a few ideas of my own," said Terry. "I'd like to talk to the witnesses, if I might." *And make sure they stick to their stories*, he added to himself.

"You can't. They all went home. Turned out that none of them were locals. They left after we interviewed them."

Ah. Good thinking on Gloria's part. "Right. I should have expected that. It's the visitors to Sulcus who want to see the Royal Park."

"Damnedest thing, though. The girl and the woman

were right near the park. The farmer was on the edge of town, on his way home. But no one in the outlying towns saw them. They seem to have vanished right outside the city."

"Bandits are good at that. Captain, I'm not sure we should concentrate all our search in one direction. I'm thinking we should spread out a bit, consider all the possible avenues of escape. I should try another route."

"So long as you don't waste your time in the north country."

"Um," said Terry. Gloria's note suddenly seemed to weigh heavier in his pocket. "The north country? Why not the north country? It's isolated. Sure, it's a long shot, but maybe someone should check it out."

"Waste of time. No bandits there. There have never been bandits there. The Old Man of the Mountains scares them off. That why I sent the Westfield kid there."

Terry had a momentary feeling of falling, the feeling you get when your horse steps into a hole and almost goes down, but then recovers. The Captain was too tired to notice his brief change of expression. "Roland Westfield?"

"Yep. Turns out he and the Princess just got engaged. Pretty bad timing, I daresay. His family bought him a brand-new fiancée and right away she disappears. Now he's financing his own search. Came over here last night trying to hire a knight to accompany him."

"Really?"

"The last thing we need is some dilettante riding out and getting himself killed over this. So I told him all the clues pointed north. It will get him safely out of the way. As long as he doesn't do something to piss off the old sorcerer, he won't get in any trouble."

"Couldn't you just order him to stay in town?"

"Not him. His people are too rich and well-connected."

"Right." Terry paced back and forth a little, thinking. He returned to the table and scrutinized the map, but he really did this so the Captain couldn't see his face. "Yes, good thinking. Send him north. Sparsely settled, with only a few roads through the mountains. With the harvest over, there's nothing going on at this time of year. It will keep him distracted for a few weeks, and then I expect he'll get bored. Still . . ." He paused thoughtfully. "You say he was looking to hire a partner?"

The Captain set down his cup and shook his head. He pushed back his chair so he could look Terry up and down. "Good Lord, Terry. You're always looking to turn a coin, aren't you? Well, can't say as I blame you, trying to keep a place in the city these days. But you're making a mistake in this case. You'll be missing out, my boy. The knight who rescues the Princess will be showered with glory. I wish I could ride out myself. Have you ever met Roland Westfield?"

"I have not. It's true I care little for glory, Captain." Terry waited to see if the Captain would object to that. When he did not, Terry continued, "But it will reflect badly on all of us if the scion of a wealthy family gets himself killed. You know how irresponsible these rich kids are. He might change his mind and ride off in a different direction. And if he can't find a real knight to go with him, he's likely to hire some thug who will lure him into a dark glen, rob him, and leave his body in a ditch. At the very least, I should see what his plans are."

The Captain tried to think about this, then decided his

brain was too fogged to argue. He shrugged. "Your choice, Terry. Here." He reached for his quill and the inkpot. "I'll write a letter of recommendation for you." Terry waited while he scrawled a reference across a sheet of foolscap, folded it, dripped it with sealing wax, and stamped it. "Here, take this. You can find him at that little bakery on Élan Street. And don't blame me if you end up guarding his clothes for him."

"Thank you, Captain." Terry took the letter and slipped it into a jacket pocket, on the opposite side from Gloria's list of instructions. "I'll let you know what I decide." He sauntered out the door, hesitating outside until he saw the Captain bend his head over his maps and papers once again. He glanced casually around to see if anyone was watching him. Then he took off for the bakery at a dead run.

For those who can afford it, the preferred means of travel between cities is the stagecoach. From the outside one can see the brightly lacquered woodwork, the high, spinning wheels, the fine teams of horses, and the liveried drivers. On the inside the traveler enjoys velvet upholstery, leather-curtained windows, and a modern suspension system that delivers a ride as smooth and comfortable as swinging in a hammock.

The drivers—former gentlemen all—are the heroes of the day, admired and emulated by men and boys alike for their style, dash, and ability to control a six-horse hitch. Their backgrounds are a mystery, their reputations much discussed. There is the dandy "Baronet" Blanco of the Bismuth line, never seen without some bit of gold on him, who supposedly took to driving after he squandered his family fortune. There is the one-eyed man known only as "The Navigator," silent and grim-faced, reputed to be a former pirate, now the champion of the Seltown–Vertebruck route. And there is the darkly handsome "Daddy" Jack Deacon, who some claim is in hiding from a string of paternity lawsuits in Alacia. Fast, skilled, and daring, they race their teams through the countryside at speeds approaching fourteen miles per hour. When the horns blow, and the gates open, and the coaches come to their stops, great joints of roasted meat, racks of savory pies, and bowls of hot spiced wine greet the hungry travelers. The inns are luxurious, the beds are soft, the food is gourmet, the company is the finest. Truly there is no more splendid way to travel the Twenty Kingdoms than by luxury stagecoach.

Gloria, however, took the mail coach.

Really, it was a good choice for the plan she had developed. Although it was slower, the mail coach actually got you where you wanted to go sooner than the fast stagecoach, because the mail coach did not stop at night. There were no meal breaks either, only a chance to grab a hot potato when the driver stopped to change horses, or throw down mail sacks. That was an advantage, too. It meant there was no demand for Gloria to answer questions about herself around a dining table. Sure, the ride was cold, rough, and uncomfortable. The coachmen wore plain postal uniforms and muddy overcoats. The windows were open, and the seats covered only with coarse wool horse blankets. But the mail coach went to places that the stagecoach did not, out-of-the-way places where the only outside news came from—well—the mail coach. By leaving Sulcus immediately, Gloria would arrive ahead of the news. By the time anyone started looking around for a missing princess, she would already be concealed on the Wayless estate.

The rough, jolting ride bounced her around, but even when the road was smooth she couldn't help bouncing a little herself, just from excitement. She was off, she was on her own, she was having an adventure! No parents, no guards, no guardians, no chaperones. Just herself and the excitement of making her own way. So what if she was cold? So what if she was hungry? She had heavy clothing, and she would reach Bornewald in a matter of days. At the end of her travails there would be love, and marriage, and—oooh!—hot, hot nights with Terry. Just thinking about it made her feel warmer. *True love and high adventure*, she reflected. It was amazing the way the two concepts fit so well together.

She was doubly fortunate in that there were no other passengers on the coach to Bornewald, for she didn't want conversation, or to attract attention. Only the coachman spoke to her, and that was but once, during a stop to water the horses. They were on a chilly mountain pass, just a few hundred feet below the snow line. Gloria wore a stylish coat of sheared beaver that she belted tightly around her slim waist, and she pulled her fur-lined hood low over her head as she hurried into the well house, knowing that the cold wind would make this attempt at concealment seem like normal behavior. Inside the well house, out of the wind, she searched for the metal dipper that usually hung on a hook inside the door. The coachman saw her and shook his head.

"There's no drinking this water, Miss. It's all right for

the horses, but it's not fit for people. It must be boiled first, to take off the curse."

Gloria looked at the well stones, then at the inside of the well house door, and then stepped outside and briefly examined the outside of the door and the lintel, searching for the spot where a wizard had made his mark. She didn't find one. She slipped back inside and pulled the door shut. "How odd," she said. "Surely the locals would hire a wizard to certify their well."

"No wizards here, Miss, nor from here on. We're in the realm of the Middle-Aged Man of the Mountains. He controls the valley, and he doesn't like competition from other wizards." The coachman made an upward gesture, which simply indicated the well house roof, although when Gloria stepped outside she looked up again. The sky was dark and low and held threats of snow, but among the swirling clouds she thought she saw a castle, perched on a distant crag.

"I'll bet he gets a great view on clear days."

"They say he sees everything, clear day or no," said the coachman. "There's a cask of cider up top, Miss, if you're thirsty."

"Thank you." Gloria dismissed the castle from her mind and drank a cup of cider. A few hours later they began the descent into the valley. It was early evening, and already dark when her trunks were unloaded at the coach station. A cold wind kept people off the streets. Gloria congratulated herself on her timing. No one was around to watch when a cart arrived to take her to the estate of Baron Wayless.

An hour later the cart turned into the drive to the Wayless estate. It traveled in the shadows of waving pine trees and emerged onto a lawn of short brown grass. In front of her was a large, country-style house, with a gray slate roof, wide chimneys, and shuttered windows, almost all of which were dark. The Baron himself, wrapped in an old bearskin coat, came out to greet her. He watched with a good deal of amusement, and a little discomfiture, as trunk after trunk was handed down. "Are you planning to throw a dinner party, my dear? How much clothing did you bring?"

"You can't wear them if you don't bring them," Gloria said cheerfully. "It may be a week before I'm rescued. I have to have something to occupy my time."

"I should have suggested bringing a book." The Baron looked sadly at the windows to his library. "I had to sell all mine, I'm afraid."

"I brought one of those, too." She remained until the last trunk was thrown down, and the cart rattled away, making sure it was out of sight before she threw back her hood. Several footmen carried away her luggage. The Baron was coughing into a handkerchief. She pretended not to notice this, waited until he had recovered, and said, "You've managed to hold on to the staff, I see. They must have faith in you."

Baron Wayless shook his head. "I haven't paid them all year. They've mostly taken jobs in the village. They help me out part-time, and in exchange they're allowed to live in their old quarters." Gloria followed him into the manor house. She could understand the seriousness of his position. Most of the rooms were closed off. Their fireplaces were cold. The walls were bare of pictures, and almost all of the furniture was gone. Everything was swept and dusted, and anything that could be polished was gleaming, but the sills needed paint, and the flower gardens had not been replanted. The Baron's coat had been carefully mended, but was still worn at the elbows. And the cuffs. And the collar. Without money, hard work can only take you so far.

Wayless led her to the dining room, where her correspondence was spread across the walnut table. "We'll destroy your own letters tonight." He lit a candle and directed its light to a neatly written confession and a handful of incriminating letters, carefully composed in his own hand. "Are you hungry, Princess? Would you care to dine before we review these?" He hardly got the words out before he doubled over in another fit of consumptive coughing. He straightened up and waved away her concern. "I'm fine, my dear. The knowledge that I will be giving Count Bussard a final shot in the eye has been like a tonic to me. And trust me, I would rather die on my feet, with a noose around my neck, than wither away in bed."

"It will be quick," Gloria admitted. This was the part of the deal that made her the most uncomfortable.

"I will wear full evening dress to my hanging," said the Baron. "I will make a speech. I will admit to the kidnapping, of course, but then I will make cryptic allusions that will have the entire country trying to find out my true motives. There will be conspiracy theories floating around for the next decade. Oh, and this is the really good part. I'll drop hints that I buried valuable family heirlooms on the estate. Even if Bussard gets control of this property again, he'll forever have to contend with fortune hunters sneaking in and digging up his gardens."

"You are a vengeful man, Baron Wayless."

"I am pleased to hear you say that, my dear." Wayless

sank into a chair. "If you only knew the misery that he has caused us. And for what? He already owns most of this valley. The richest land, the clearest streams, the most valuable timber are his. But no, he has to have it all, and he uses any means, fair or foul, to get it."

Gloria was relieved. Her biggest fear during the trip to Bornewald was that the Baron would get cold feet and renege on his agreement. Instead, he was downright cheerful as he showed her the evidence against himself, then folded the letters neatly into a file folder and left it in plain sight on the sideboard. "You can direct their attention to it if they fail to look at it, my dear. You would be surprised how many investigators will tell you that it is ungentlemanly to read another man's mail, even in the line of duty."

The Princess nodded. Fortunately, women were not subject to this compunction. "I don't want to dissuade you, Baron Wayless, but I must be perfectly honest. When you are arrested for the kidnapping, of course your property will be forfeit to the king."

"Of course."

"You realize that if other people hold liens on your land, and my father seizes it, they may go to court and demand compensation. Depending on how influential they are, and what sort of mood my father is in, he may grant it."

"Ha!" The Baron was gleeful. "Yes! The king might pay compensation, but it will be on the taxable value. And Bussard has the tax office under his thumb. He's made sure that the assessed value is a fraction of what it is really worth. He won't get spit in compensation. Hoist by his own petard. Oh, the poetic justice of it all. Too bad I won't be around to see it." He darted away into the next room. Gloria heard an extended fit of coughing, but when he came back the Baron was smiling. He had a fresh handkerchief in one hand and a dusty bottle in the other. "Port wine," he said. "The last bottle in the cellar. My wife and I got a case of it as a gift when I inherited this estate. Now we will bring it all to a finish. Will you do me the honor of having a glass with me, Princess Gloria?"

"Thank you, Baron Wayless. I'd love a glass."

"I'm not opposed to sliced bread, myself," Terry said. "I like sliced bread. It's just that I think it ought to be clearly labeled as sliced, so the consumer can make an informed choice."

"But sliced bread is exactly the same as broken bread," objected Roland. "It's just been sliced."

"Then there's no reason it shouldn't be labeled as such." said Terry. "Stop." They had come to a place where the road forked. Both trails narrowed past the fork, and wound into deep woods, where the bare branches of thin black trees whipped in the cool breeze. They had not seen another traveler all day. They were a long way from the city, several days hard ride, and this part of Medulla did not get a lot of commerce, at least not at this time of year. Terry got off his horse. He was a big man, but he rode a big, stolid warhorse, easily a full hand taller than Roland's spirited racer. He waited while Roland settled his horse, then got down on one knee.

"Check the hoof marks," he said, pointing to the hard-packed dirt. "They're faint, I know, but you can see that this horseshoe has three nails with round heads and two nails with square heads. That's one of the horses we've been following. It went left. So we can take the left fork."

Roland studied the ground where Terry pointed, but he couldn't see any difference between it and the adjoining patches of ground, because there wasn't any. While he was looking down, Terry pulled a scrap of lace from his pocket and let it flutter away in the breeze.

Roland stood up and brushed the dirt from his stylish new riding clothes. "Amazing. I'll have to take your word for it, Terry. My tracking skills are no match for yours."

"It just takes practice," Terry assured him. They mounted up again and turned their horses down the left fork. But Terry stopped his horse after only a few paces. "There!" A cluster of thornbushes grew beside the road. He swung down, darted to one of them, and plucked a small piece of white cloth from its branches. He showed it to Roland.

"What is it?"

"Lace. It's been torn from Princess Gloria's dress."

Roland looked at the thornbush with concern. "Is she injured, do you think?"

Terry shook his head and pocketed the square again before Roland could look at it too closely. "No, I think she tore it off herself. This is not the first piece I've seen. I thought that piece might have torn off by accident. But now I think she is dropping them on purpose, to leave a trail for us."

Roland nodded. "A brave girl," he said, as Terry mounted his horse. "And clever, too. If it is from her dress, it verifies that we're on the right trail. But what makes you think it's from Princess Gloria's dress?"

"Because it's lace." Terry got his horse started down the road. "Gloria loves lace. I know, they're all wearing lace now—it's the fashionable thing—but with the Princess Gloria it's kind of a signature look."

"I didn't know that. Was she wearing a dress with lace that day? I'm afraid I don't move in court circles."

"Gloria? Of course she was. She wears lace all the time. I don't know how you could miss it."

"I've never seen her."

"What?" Terry was astonished. "You're engaged to a girl you've never seen?"

"That's correct. It will be an arranged marriage."

"Sure, but didn't you at least try to get a look at her? Demand an introduction from her family, or cadge an invitation to one of her parties? Aren't you curious? What if you don't like her?"

"What's the point? I have a responsibility to my family. I'm going to marry her, no matter what. If not her, someone else of their choosing. I've got things to do. I can't go around meeting every girl in town. If she is attractive, it will be a pleasant surprise. If she is unattractive, why torture myself with the knowledge? I don't even want to know what she is like. It's better just to go into this with an open mind."

"I guess," Terry conceded reluctantly.

"She's never met me either."

"Huh. You can bet she knows everything about you."

"Oh."

They rode in silence for another mile. Then Roland said, "Um, so what does she look like?"

She is a vision of beauty, Terry thought. The words came to mind, immediate and unbidden. *She moves like a ripple on a summer lake. Her hair floats about her in a soft golden cloud, gently blown by hidden winds. The light of her smile will dispel the darkness in your heart, and the warmth of her touch will kindle the fire in your soul. She looks totally killer in high heels and stockings.* He knew, however, that this was not the kind of description a smart man gave to a potential rival, so he just said, "She looks okay."

Roland reflected on this. They climbed through a narrow pass, where a cold wind took their breath away. Conversation stopped. Terry kept one hand near his sword, since any narrow pass is a good place for road agents. There were not supposed to be bandits in this part of the country, but it had been several years since he had last been this way, and things might have changed. They didn't see anyone, however, and once they were through the pass, the wind dropped off, and a pleasant, cultivated valley spread out before them. The fields were bare, because it was after the harvest, but cattle grazed at hay bales, and horses nosed around the base of apple and pear trees, looking for windfalls. It made a surprising change from the rough, rocky hills, and the unsettled forests that they had been riding through. The small village of Bornewald, with its cluster of thatched buildings, lay in their path. "She's beautiful."

"Hmm?" Terry looked around. "Who?"

"The Princess Gloria. She must be beautiful. A princess in the Twenty Kingdoms is always beautiful. There's nothing to worry about. And she's probably a very nice person, too. Right?"

"Sure," said Terry.

"She isn't a redhead, is she?"

"No."

Roland looked at him suspiciously. "She doesn't do anything like, say, talk to smoked hams?"

"Not that I've heard." They were close enough to the village that Terry could point to an inn. "But while we're on the subject of food, I suggest we stop to eat there."

"You don't want to keep on? We can't be too far behind them."

"This is the end of the coach road. From here on it's just horse trail and footpaths. It's too easy to lose them in the dark. Besides, this part of the country is rarely visited. They'll probably consider themselves safe here. I suspect they will also settle in for the night. But the important thing is that I've got some connections in this village. I want to talk with them and hear if they have any information about a bandit hideout."

For a small place in a small village in a rural, barely accessible valley, the inn did a pretty good business, for it had the advantage of being the only public place on the road, as well as the end of the line for the monthly coach. The dining room was cheerily lit by a crackling fire, and full of the smell of roasting meat, baking pies, and woodsmoke. Two young girls in aprons tended the tables and bar. When they weren't busy they cast their eyes toward Roland and whispered to each other. Terry caught a glimpse of another girl through the kitchen door, one who was slim and pretty, with her hair tucked under a chef's toque. The menu was posted on a large piece of black slate. Both men were surprised at how elaborate it was. They were expecting the usual country fare of stews, soups, sausage, and perhaps mutton, but it also had a selection of fish, local game, and baked goods.

"The wine is also good," said Roland. He sipped his glass approvingly. "It's not often you find good wine from these local vineyards. And these girls know how to serve it properly. Will you try it?"

"I prefer cider," said Terry, who did not. He did like good wine, in fact, but usually he couldn't afford it.

"Jam tarts and jam rolls," murmured Roland, half to himself. "Always happens this time of year. The local farms put up too much jam, and they can't get rid of it. Hmm, poached cod."

"Surely you're not going to order cod this far inland? It's going to be dried."

"Dried fish can actually be quite tasty if poached properly and served with a béchamel sauce," said Roland, although he eventually ordered the pheasant pie. Terry ordered sausage. It was the cheapest thing on the menu. The dragon-slaying expedition had cut seriously into his finances, and this trip wasn't improving them.

It was an age before travel for recreation had become popular, and strangers in small towns were often greeted with suspicion. Had Roland been on his own, he might even have been jailed as a fugitive, a miscreant, or worse, a traveling salesman. He knew this. That was why he had sought assistance from the Captain of the Royal Guard. Terry's coat of arms made sure that doors stayed open for them.

Terry was traveling with Roland as a companion in arms. Roland had first offered to hire him as an assistant and guide. When Terry declined payment, Roland offered to pay his expenses. Terry respectfully declined that also, explaining to Roland that he could not possibly accept compensation for doing his duty to his king and country.

The truth was that he couldn't take Roland's coin. If he did, he would be working for Roland, everything he did would be on Roland's behalf, and that included rescuing Gloria. He would have to maintain strict independence if he wanted to marry Gloria. It would still be dishonorable to take his companion's girl, but there was no way around that. He told himself that he was doing Gloria's bidding. That certainly outweighed any obligation he had to Roland. Gloria was, after all, a princess of Medulla, while Roland, although wealthy, was still merely the son of a merchant. It was simply a question of social rank.

Terry became aware that Roland was asking him a question. "Hmm?"

"I was wondering what made you decide to become a knight?"

"Oh well, you know how it goes. When you're the biggest kid around, the adults give you all the responsibility. They want you to look after the other kids and keep them out of danger. And I just sort of fell naturally into knighthood. I guess I grew up to think of myself as someone who went around defending the weak, protecting the poor, and upholding the king's law."

"That sounds very noble, Terry."

"Thank you."

"Also totally unbelievable. What's the real reason?"

"To score with girls. The babes go wild for a man in shining armor."

"That I can believe."

"And how about yourself? I take it you're following along in the family footsteps?"

"Pretty much. It all began with my great-grandfather. He invented a process for making microchips."

"That must have been difficult."

"Well, you have to start with very small potatoes. And the family has been into cookery ever since."

Terry slid his chair away from the table. "Excuse me. I need to meet my informants. I won't be long."

Roland nodded. "I'll go with you."

"Ah, that's not a good idea. They don't know you. They won't talk in front of you. It's better if you stay here and watch the door." He looked around the room, indicating the other diners with his eyes. "Tell me if anyone seems to follow me out."

"Right." Roland pulled out his money pouch. "Take some silver. Tell them we're willing to pay for information."

It was tempting, but Terry waved it away. "No need. The crown will reimburse me for the expense if we are successful." Roland shrugged and put his money away. Terry rose, and, with feigned casualness, left through the front door. Taking care that he could not be seen through the dining room windows, he walked around to the back of the inn, where he found a fenced in yard with an un-latched gate. He let himself in and settled on a stack of firewood for a moderately long wait. The night was clear, so the temperature was already dropping. The fence helped to block the wind. Through the trees, he noted the position of the crescent moon. He made a mental vow not to go back inside until it rose above a certain branch, so he wouldn't return too soon.

Bored, he rubbed his ears to warm them up while he looked around the woodlot. It had the usual wood-chopping hardware—an ax, a sledgehammer, and a couple of iron wedges. Driven by male instinct, he picked up the ax and hammer in turn and hefted each one. Putting them back down, he found half a dozen long-handled objects leaning against the fence. He examined one of them. It was made of black iron, with a wooden handle and a long stem. It looked rather like a fork for toasting sausages around a campfire, except that against the fork was a flat wire grill. Curious, he took it by the handle and waved it around his head, wondering if it was some kind of weapon, or a flyswatter for really tough bugs.

He jumped a little when the back door opened. The cook came out, smiled at him, and took off her hat. She was pretty enough with it on, but when her long hair fell around her shoulders she looked especially lovely. "Hello," she said. "Can I help you with something?"

"Just getting a bit of air," said Terry.

"I see you've found the toasting forks."

Terry held up the implement of destruction. "This?"

"Yep. They're my own invention. I used them for toasting sliced bread." She went to the fence, where bundles of garlic and dried peppers were strung between the posts, and plucked some off. "I know it seems silly, but the customers like it."

"Toasted bread?" Terry examined the fork again. "Why? Why would you want to toast bread?"

"Well, we like to serve sliced bread here. It's convenient and makes for easier portion control. A lot of the customers still didn't trust it, though. But we managed to convince them that searing sliced bread with fire makes it safe to eat. You know, sort of like the belief that boiling water makes it safe to drink? Everybody became happy with toasted bread. Now most of our customers won't even eat sliced bread unless it is toasted."

"Don't you boil your drinking water here?"

"Oh, we have to, because the customers want it, but I think it's kind of silly myself. There's no evidence that boiling water makes it safe to drink. It's just another one of those superstitions." The girl finished gathering peppers. "I hope you enjoy your meal. If you're going to stay out much longer, feel free to keep warm by chopping firewood."

Terry watched her go back inside. Smiling, he chopped some kindling, then searched the woodpile for a hickory log, always a difficult wood to split. He found one of medium size, put it on the chopping block, and cracked it with the ax. He set the wedge into the crack, picked up the sledgehammer, and swung it over his shoulder. A glance at the moon told him it was time to go back inside. Almost absently, he brought the hammer down with one hand. The log cleaved neatly in two. He returned all the tools to their storage places and went back inside to find Roland.

His companion was finishing dessert. "The cook did a good job with the pie crust on that pheasant. So I wanted to see what she could do with a custard."

"How was it?"

"Excellent. And the coffee is first-rate."

"Good. We've found the Princess."

Roland sat up. "Yes? Where?"

"Keep your voice down."

Roland looked around the room. One of the waitresses smiled at him. The other diners had finished eating and were now clustered over at the bar. He hunched his chair closer to the table. "Where is she?"

"She is stashed at a local manor. Our kidnappers are in the pay of a certain Baron Wayless. Apparently he's deeply in debt and desperate for money."

"The fiend. What's our plan, Terry? Do we get her now? Steal in under cover of night?"

Terry shook his head. "Not now. We don't have enough information. I've sent my man back to scout out the manor. He says he knows a servant who may let him inside."

"That will be fortunate for us."

"Very fortunate. I'll ride out with him tonight and survey the grounds."

"I'll come with you."

"I afraid you can't. He doesn't want to reveal himself to you. The best thing you can do, Roland, is to have a few drinks at the bar here." Terry nodded in the direction of the bar. "Keep your ears open and listen for any of the locals discussing Baron Wayless. Listen for news of any strangers in town. Besides us, of course. See if these girls will talk to you. A lot of good information is picked up that way."

"Right," said Roland. "I'll be good at that."

"Then go to bed early. I'll wake you when I return. We'll work out a plan of attack."

Roland nodded. The young waitress brought over their bill, leaning close to Roland as she presented it to him. Roland reached for his money again. "Dinner's on me."

"No," said Terry firmly. "We'll split it."

"You're an independent cuss, aren't you, Terry?"

"I'm afraid so." Terry counted out some coins from his vanishing supply. He gave them to the girl with a bright smile. Inwardly, he sighed.

Alison entered the manor house through the garden door, wearing a housecoat over her kitchen dress and apron. She had a basket of rolls from the restaurant hanging from one arm, and from the other, a string bag heavy with parsnips, carrots, and onions. In one pocket of her coat she had a bottle of wine, and in the other, a soup bone wrapped in butcher paper. She took the food to the kitchen and flexed her arms to get the cramps out of her muscles. It was a long walk from the inn. Normally she stayed in the village, sleeping in the kitchen with the other girls, but she made a point to go home at least twice a week and check on her father. She also knew that once the snows came this would be more difficult. She thought again about trying to get him to move into town. But where would he stay? They had no money to spare. His pride would not let him take a cheap room at a mere pub. On the rare occasions he visited Sulcus, he had stayed at a gentlemen's club.

She was able to locate him easily by the sound of his coughing. He was sitting at the dining table, hunched over. He did most of his work in the dining room these days, taking advantage of the warmth from the kitchen. He had a very nice office upstairs, with large windows that afforded an excellent view of the land they no longer owned. He had even kept the furniture. But he couldn't afford to keep another fire going. He didn't straighten up when she kissed the back of his neck. "I'll make you some tea and honey, Papa. It will soothe your throat."

"Thank you, dear. But no thank you. The coughing is not from the throat, it's from the lungs."

"And I'm making soup."

"Thank you, but I'm not hungry."

"You must eat anyway, to keep up your strength."

"Fortunately I won't have to keep it up for much

longer." The Baron turned around in his chair. "Alison, dear, please remember that I have asked you not to wear your restaurant clothes to the house. I may not have money, but I still have my pride."

Alison took her chef's toque out of her pocket and put it on his head. He smiled ruefully. "There is nothing wrong with working, Papa. Many fine people work."

"Not the best people. It is bad enough when a man must work to support himself. It is even worse when his daughter must work."

"I don't mind it."

"I wouldn't mind it either if you didn't need to do it. That's the embarrassing part."

"That's why they call it work. If you don't need to do it, it isn't work. It's a hobby."

"I can't believe you really like being a kitchen drudge."

"I didn't say I liked it. I said I didn't mind it. And I am certainly not a kitchen drudge. I'm the cook. I have two kitchen drudges reporting to me. And there's nothing undignified about working. The nobility should try it, Papa. Most people do work, you know."

"Most people still respect the nobility, my dear."

Alison wrinkled her nose. "Ha! Which people? The tools of the ruling class. If the proletariat would throw off the shackles of materialism and rebel against their en-slavement by the so-called nobility, they would . . ."

"My dear, please remember that you are talking to a member of the so-called nobility. A position you will in-herit in the not-too-distant future."

"Um, right. Right. Sorry. You spend all day working with drudges and it kind of gets to you after a while.

Anyway, you just sit here and rest, while I cook up some soup. Soup is good for you. It's easy to digest. And the hot liquid will help unclog your lungs." She went through the swinging door into the kitchen. The Baron was seated at the end of the table, near the door, so he could still hear her while she talked and chopped things.

"The coach came in," she said through the door. "I brought the mail and the news from the city."

"Thank you. Anything good?"

"No, not really. Just a lot of court gossip. And two strangers came to town. They're staying at the inn. I think they might be working for Bussard."

"Really?" Baron Wayless turned in his chair. "What makes you say that?"

"Just a hunch. I saw one of them standing outside the back door, like he was waiting for someone. A big, tough-looking sort of guy. I don't know. He just looked like he was here to cause trouble."

The Baron made a mental note to ask Gloria what her rescuer was supposed to look like. "Two strangers, you said."

"The girls told me there were two. I didn't get a chance to go up front and see. It was a busy night. You know how it is at the inn. It's always busy these first few days after the coach comes in, when everyone comes to the village to pick up their mail."

"Yes, of course."

"I'll bring you the newspaper as soon as I get these onions off my hands. It says a princess was kidnapped."

This time Wayless turned so quickly his neck joint made a cracking noise. The motion triggered another coughing fit. When he finally got his lungs under control, and was able to listen again, he realized that Alison had kept on talking. ". . . anytime there's anything strange going on around here, you can bet Count Bussard has his hand in it somehow." The sound of chopping became audibly more vicious. "And I'm sure he's in cahoots with the Middle-Aged Man of the Mountains, although of course everyone is too frightened to talk about him. The commoners suffer the most. If the workers would just unite, they would have the power to stand up to their oppressors." Alison came through the swinging door and looked at her father with her hands on her hips. "Papa, I don't know why you don't write to the king. I'm sure he'd set things to right if he knew."

"For the same reason that no one else complains, my dear. Fear of retaliation. There's no way to send a message without Bussard learning who sent it."

"Don't you think the king would protect you?"

"Bussard collects the taxes and sends the king his proper share. He's the man the king will listen to." In his mind, Wayless gave a wry chuckle. He wanted to do it out loud, but was afraid it would trigger more coughing. "But fear not, my dear. There are other ways to attract the king's attention, even to our little village of Bornewald."

Alison shot him a speculative look, but apparently decided to talk about it another time. She vanished back into the kitchen. There was the sound of pots and pans being moved about, and water being drawn from the cistern. A few minutes later she came out again with a basket of rolls in her hands and a broadsheet under her arm. She ran straight into Gloria.

"Um," Alison said, but it was a word that spoke volumes. She was not mentally prepared for this. Had it been daylight—teatime perhaps, her brain might have adjusted to sight of a girl with curly blond hair, fashionably clothed in a new wine-colored dress with black lace sleeves, standing by her father's chair. She might have assumed the girl dropped by for a social visit. But it was well after dark, and the only reasons she could imagine for a beautiful girl at her father's side were too ridiculous to even consider. So she simply stopped and stared.

"Oh, is that the Sulcus newspaper?" said Gloria, slipping it away from her. "May I see this? Thank you."

"Um," said Alison.

It was a moment that Baron Wayless knew would come, but one he had been hoping, right up until the last minute, that he could avoid. Now he rose, a bit stiffly, bowed to Gloria, and said formally, "Princess Gloria, allow me to present my daughter Alison. Alison, this is the Princess Gloria."

"Delighted," said Gloria.

"Um," said Alison. Acting on autopilot, her hands lifted her skirt and she began a formal curtsey. But she stopped halfway down and straightened up again. "Right," she said. "Yeah, right. Princess Gloria. Papa, who is this?"

The Baron coughed. This time it was not a real cough, but one of those discreet I-need-time-to-think coughs. "This really is the Princess Gloria, my dear. She will be staying with us for a few days. As you see, she has not exactly been kidnapped."

"Not exactly been kidnapped? How, Papa, do you *not exactly* kidnap a princess? She's either kidnapped or she isn't."

"I kidnapped myself," explained Gloria. "Although

your father certainly helped," she added, wanting to give credit where it was due.

"There's a story behind it," said the Baron. "It's rather amusing, in a way." He proceeded to describe the plan, with help from Gloria, to Alison, who started out unamused and grew less and less so with each sentence. Still, she managed to keep her temper until almost the end of the story, at which point she exploded.

"You'll be executed!"

The Baron was one of those men who grew calmer when people around him got excited. "Yes, my dear. That is rather the idea. I'm dying already. We've both learned to accept that."

"You'll be arrested! You'll spend the rest of your life in prison!"

"That won't be very long. Hardly enough to make it worth packing a change of clothes."

"You don't know that! You might live a long time yet! Some people with your condition have lived months longer. Years, even."

"Lingering on in pain and febrility. True, I was looking forward to that. But I think I can handle the disappointment."

"Pain? You'll die in pain, Papa. Are you forgetting that? You'll be tortured. It will be far worse than any natural death."

"Not at all, my dear. I won't be tortured. I'll confess to everything."

"A cure might be discovered. You don't know! It could happen tomorrow."

"What a wonderful thought. My life will be spared so I can spend it in debtors' prison."

Alison strove to lower her voice, to adopt a tone that
was calm and reasonable. "Papa," she said soothingly,
"you are a fine man. You've led a good life. Is this the
kind of legacy you want to leave behind? Do you want to
be remembered as a criminal?"

"As a matter of fact, I do. You're still young, my dear,
and you don't understand how men think. We'd all much
rather be remembered as scoundrels and rogues than as
paupers and failures."

"What of your estate? It will be confiscated. Everything we have will be taken!"

"Everything we have is mortgaged. At least this way it
will go to the king and not Count Bussard.

"It's a stupid and futile plan. The land will be put up
for sale. Bussard will get it anyway."

"Perhaps. But you, my dear, will at last be free of
debt."

Alison gave him a withering stare. "Surely you're not
going to claim that you are doing this for me? You will
not only lose your life and estate, you'll lose your title,
your reputation, and your good name. And so will I, inci-
dentally." She decided to elaborate on this. "Yes, Papa. If
you won't think of yourself, think of me, your daughter.
When you're gone, Papa, I'll be all alone in the world. I'll
have nothing."

"No," said Gloria. "I'll take care of that. It's part of
deal. I have a lawyer arranging it now."

"It's your chance to get free of all this, Alison. Make a
fresh start in a new city."

"It's disloyal to the king," snapped Alison, trying a
new tactic. "If he chose some rich guy for her husband,
then that's the man she should marry." She pointed a fin-

ger at Gloria. "Women do not have the right to choose their own husbands. That's for their parents to decide. It's her duty to obey her father and it's your duty to support the king."

"You rejected every suitor I ever chose for you," said her father mildly.

"That's not the same!" Alison's voice was shrill. "This is completely different!"

Gloria realized it was time to retreat. She nodded to the Baron and quietly slipped outside the door. The Baron pulled another chair away from the table. "Alison, my dear, please sit down."

"I'm not . . ."

"Sit down," said the Baron, gently but firmly. "Let's talk about this calmly."

Alison sat down sullenly, with her arms folded across her breasts. Wayless uncrossed them and held her hands in his. "Alison, if your mother were alive . . ."

Alison snatched her hands away. "Don't bring Mother into this! That is so unfair!"

"I promised her I would take care of you," the Baron pressed on. "She lived her whole life with me under this crushing burden of debt. I inherited it from my father and he from his father, and I should have known we would never get out from under it. I should not even have proposed to her. But we were young and foolish and we were in love and we thought anything was possible. Then we had you, and we saw the world differently."

"We were happy," said Alison, although not with conviction.

"Bussard's shadow loomed over us," said her father. "It still does. He will never leave us, and so you must leave him. Alison, all your mother wanted was for you to be free of this."

Alison was silent for long minutes. Eventually she said, "What do you want me to do?"

"Go to the city. You don't have to marry if it won't make you happy. The Princess will get you a position. Something with dignity. Possibly even something at the palace. You will move in court circles. Go to parties. Go to the Autumn Ball. Meet boys your own age. Have fun. Enjoy life while you are still young."

"All right! All right, Papa, you can count on my support. But I'm not leaving you while you're still alive. And if there is a trial, I'm standing beside you until it is over."

"Agreed," said the Baron. He leaned back in his chair. "Then let us put this conversation behind us and enjoy some of the excellent soup you are making."

"I brought some bread from the inn."

Alison stood up, but before she could leave Gloria popped her head in the door. "Is everything settled?" She looked at their faces and beamed. "Terrific. Come on." She pushed the door wide open and grabbed Alison by the hand. "Let's go and try on some clothes."

In these enlightened times, the giving of a woman's hand in marriage as a reward for valiant or chivalrous feats might seem a bit insensitive, if not downright uncivilized. Gloria herself had been heard to criticize the practice as an obsolete relic of a barbarous past. But it was a tradition that was entwined in the very roots of history, at least in the Twenty Kingdoms.

One of the earliest stories concerning the matter was

recorded in the country of Alacia, when a young man in highly polished armor took up a post on the bridge over the Obitron River, and declared that any man who wished to pass over it must first defeat him in combat. It so happened that the ruler of Alacia, Queen Betty IV, was attending a garden party in the nearby town of Demesne. She sent her minister to inquire of the young man, in words that have come down through the centuries, "What the hell are you doing, you idiot?"

The young man dismounted, knelt before the minister, and gave him this story to take back to the queen. His name was Gaston DuNeasy. He had fallen in love with a very beautiful lady, to whom he had pledged his free will. She demanded that he wear an iron collar around his neck and apparently serve her in other ways that historians found too indelicate to record. After two years his ardor cooled, or perhaps he suffered an attack of good sense, and begged that the lady release him from his oath. Smirking, she said that she would release him if he could break thirty lances in thirty days. He proposed to turn aside every man or woman who attempted to cross until they could find a champion to defeat him.

The minister carried this message to the queen, who was not amused. The road was important to Alacian trade. She called together her cadre of knights and explained the situation. They agreed, once they had stopped snickering at Gaston's predicament, that they could remove him from the bridge with no problem.

At this point most histories go into long and flowery descriptions of shining steel, charging stallions, and flashing lances. Here, let it suffice to say that Gaston performed the remarkable feat of breaking seventeen lances in twelve days, an act of chivalry unsurpassed in the Twenty Kingdoms. By that time he was also battered and broken to the point where he could not continue. The town elders were concerned—they said it would be bad for business if such a gallant young man died on their turf. Queen Betty took stock of the situation and declared that seventeen was equal to thirty, by royal decree, for this day only, and she had a nice solid dungeon ready for any mathematician who had a problem with the idea. No one objected. With great ceremony the collar was removed. Gaston, under the queen's stern eye, was sent hobbling down the road. Seventeen knights returned to their wives and girlfriends, each to explain that he could have beaten Gaston anytime, really, but just felt sorry for the kid.

And here the story should have reached its rightful end, were it not for the fact that two years later Gaston DuNeasy returned, this time sporting leather underwear, pierced nipples, and a tale about a kinky babe named Lisa to whom he had pledged his troth. Queen Betty, never long on patience to begin with, did not send her knights to combat Gaston. She sent one knight, and an inexperienced one at that. When he was defeated she sent for the lady in question, handed her a wedding veil, a bouquet of flowers, and a fondue set, and had her married on the spot to Gaston, after which she ordered the couple to forever stay out of her sight and shut up about their damn sex life.

Okay, so it's not a great story, and certainly not romantic, but Queen Betty helped establish a precedent that a lady's hand in marriage could indeed be awarded to a knight for an act of courage. Her actions have been cited in hundreds of court cases throughout the Twenty Kingdoms.

Gloria wasn't just indulging a fantasy when she put together her plan. She knew it would work.

Terry laid the sketch on the table, using a candlestick and an inkwell to hold down the corners. Roland studied it carefully. It showed the various rooms of the manor house, with the door and windows marked. "That's a pretty good sketch. Your man did a hell of a job."

"Um, yes. He's been inside before this." They were in Terry's room at the inn. It held a bed, a cupboard, and a round table with four chairs. Terry suspected the room was used for card games. But it was convenient for their plans. He had shaken Roland awake in the early morning, before the sun was up, so he could pretend he had been out reconnoitering. He half expected to find one of the girls from the kitchen with Roland, and was a little surprised that he was sleeping alone. Roland woke quickly and followed him to the other room. A single candle burned on the table. The windows were shuttered. Downstairs, all was quiet. They kept their voices low.

"Do you have confidence in him, Terry? Do you think this sketch is accurate?"

"I'm absolutely sure of it," said Terry. And he was. Baron Wayless had drawn the sketch himself and sent it to Gloria, who had sent it on to Terry before she slipped out of Sulcus. "We'll leave here before dawn, wait in the woods outside the manor, and go in at first light. The bandits have been drinking, my man said, so they won't be easily roused. We probably won't even see them."

"Why do we wait until light? Wouldn't it be better to go in now? Under cover of darkness?"

Terry shook his head. "They may pursue us, and we'll have to ride fast. We can't do that at night. We don't know the roads, and the horses might stumble." Actually Terry didn't know why they were entering at dawn—only that Gloria told him she would wait for an hour each morning in the kitchen, and to plan his rescue for that time. "And we don't know what room she is in. We'll need to search for her. We can't do that in the dark."

"How will I recognize her? Are there any other women in the house?"

"According to my man, no. No women are staying as guests, or family members. If there are any maids, they will be in uniform. And the princess is wearing a blue dress." This wasn't true either. Terry knew that Gloria disliked blue.

Roland nervously pulled his sword half out of the scabbard and put it back in. Terry guessed what he was thinking. "Don't try to fight off a gang, Roland. Just back away and use the sword to cover your retreat."

"Right."

"Okay." Terry pulled his chair up to the table and marked the map with a bit of charcoal. "The main entrance is in the center here, with the grand staircase. Bedrooms are on the second floor. She's most likely to be in one of them. Here's the rose garden with patio doors on the east side, and another staircase, and here is the kitchen on the west, with a service stairs. The stairs are undoubtedly going to creak, but there's nothing we can do about that. Just go slowly. The upstairs hall is carpeted, so that will help us move more quietly."

The drawing showed a kitchen and a small family dining room at one end of the house, separated from the formal dining room by a breezeway. Since fires were most likely to start in the kitchen, this design reduced the chance that one would spread to the rest of the house. He drew Roland's attention to this part of the sketch. "You enter through there, the kitchen entrance, up the stairs, and search the rooms from west to east. I'll come in through the patio doors and search the bedrooms on that side. We'll meet at the top of the grand staircase. If we haven't found her, we'll search the lower floors." This was a bit of craftiness on Terry's part. It was going to be tricky, to bring Roland along and still make sure that Terry could claim full credit for rescuing Gloria. Unconsciously, he held his breath.

"Ah," said Roland. He looked uncomfortable.

"Yes, Roland?" Terry said innocently. "Feel free to make any suggestions."

"Well, it's just that . . . I'm supposed to . . ." He cleared his throat. "You expect me to go in through a *servant's* entrance?"

"Oh, right. Of course. Sorry." Terry pretended to think for a moment. "I'll tell you what. You go in through the rose garden, and I'll go in through the kitchen. Same plan, just different directions."

"You don't mind?"

"Not at all. Now, if you find the princess, take her with you and leave immediately. Don't wait for me. The important thing to do is get her out of there. Of course, if I find her, I'll do the same thing."

"Of course." Roland adjusted his cuffs. Terry had told him to dress in dark clothing, so he was wearing a black silk shirt, black breeches, and polished black boots. The shirt had silver buttons, his belt a silver buckle, and even the boots were tipped with gleaming silver, all of which negated the point of wearing black, but Terry let it pass. It wasn't a real attack, and they weren't going in under cover of darkness. He just wanted to see what Roland would come up with. And, he had to admit, the man looked pretty sharp. Terry wished he had brought some snappier shirts for himself. He was dressed in woodland colors, dark green and brown. He found himself hoping that Gloria would not see Roland.

"All right, then." He folded the map. "Are we ready?" Roland nodded. "Then let's ride."

Like Terry and Roland, Gloria and Alison did not get much in the way of sleep. They hadn't intended to stay up all night, but they had tried on some outfits, and that, of course, meant they had to try on some jewelry, and that, of course, meant they had to change their makeup, then they had opened up the bottle of wine, and in between chatting, and putting up their hair, and taking it down again, they discovered that they both wore the same size shoes, so of course they had to try those on, which meant changing outfits again, and pretty soon Alison's closets were emptied, and the contents of Gloria's trunks were spread across the bed. And at that point they noticed that the sky was getting lighter, and it would soon be dawn.

"It's going to be today," Gloria said. "I can feel it. I just know he's going to come for me today."

"Why so early? Do rescues always take place at dawn?" Alison was lacing up Gloria's dress in the back. "If I was going to be rescued from a gang of murderous brigands, I would schedule it for the evening. Then we could go somewhere afterward and have a drink. You know, make a date of it. And why the kitchen?" She tied off the laces in a bow. "There. Turn around and let me see."

It was a lovely pink-and-cream number with gathered sleeves. Gloria did a slow pirouette. "He has to be seen. I want there to be witnesses that he rescued me. That way there will be no doubt that he's won my hand in marriage. Your father told me that the kitchen will be the busiest place in the morning. People will be dropping off milk and produce and firing the stove."

"Yes, there should be a few people around. You don't think this is a bit too dressy for a rescue? Shouldn't a kidnapped victim looked a bit more—I don't know—harassed?"

"I'm thinking that we might stop at a small chapel somewhere and get married on the way back. Roland's family might try to contest the marriage. Miligras says that if we present the court with a *fait accompli*, it will be much more difficult to undo."

"But don't you want a big wedding? A big dress with a long trail, and candles, and an orchestra, and a seven-tiered wedding cake?"

"Of course I do. But what is love if a girl is not willing to make sacrifices? Anyway, half the reason we have big weddings is to make our mothers happy. And my mother is not going to be happy about this one, no matter what I wear."

"Oh, this is lovely." Alison took the last dress from the bottom of one of Gloria's trunks. It was pale blue, a simple sheath of watered silk, with spaghetti straps. She held it against herself and looked in the mirror.

Gloria glanced at it. "You like it? You can have it."

"No. Really? No, I couldn't possibly."

"I don't care for the color. Try it on."

"It would set off your eyes."

"It's too cold. With my blond hair and blue eyes and pale skin? A little blue is okay, but a whole dress will make me look icy. When my boyfriend sees me . . ." Here Gloria cocked a hip in a saucy manner and ran her tongue lasciviously across her lips. "I like to look *hot.*"

Alison giggled. "You are so bad."

The princess looked out the window. "It's time for me to go downstairs. Try on the dress, Alison. I'm sure it will look much better on you than me. If I'm not rescued today, I'll be back in an hour. But don't count on it."

"Do you want me to go down with you? I can be a witness."

"No, you need to stay away. We'll want to testify that you had no involvement or knowledge of the plot at all. If anyone asks questions of you, you'll say you were asleep in bed the whole time. So you stay tucked up here, away from the action. Terry will come in, confront your father, there will be a little swordplay . . ." She saw Alison's look of concern. "Just pretend swordplay. The Baron won't get hurt. And then my knight in shining armor will carry me off to safety. In a manner of speaking."

"A romantic tale that will carry down through the ages," Alison said straight-faced. "Ballads will be written about the pair of you. I hope you two have fun. If I don't see you for a while, take my best wishes with you."

"Thank you." Gloria slung her bag over her shoulder and ran down the stairs. She really did have a very good feeling about today. At the bottom of the stairs she even had to stop herself from skipping. Down the hallway, past the empty rooms and closed door, across the breezeway. She went into the dining room. The Baron was lying on the floor.

"Oh my God!" Gloria fell to her knees beside him. He was unconscious but breathing. She felt his pulse. It was strong and steady. She sighed with relief.

She wondered what happened. Had Terry come in and been too rough with him? Or did he pass out from a coughing fit? She took a seat cushion, put it under the Baron's head, and went into the kitchen to look for help. Another man, a laborer, was sitting against the wall. Blood was dripping from his jaw. His eyes were closed. She grabbed a towel and looked for the cistern to soak it. Not seeing it, she edged out the back door. "Terry?" She caught a quick glimpse of a man on horseback, before someone behind her put a sack over her head.

A rough male voice said, "Lie down quietly, and you won't get hurt." Gloria screamed and kicked out. "Ow!" the man said. "Goddammit!" She flailed her fists blindly and connected with someone's face. The response was more cursing, but she didn't wait to hear the full repertoire. She backed into the kitchen, grappled with the sack, and finally tore it free. A man in uniform, young, fair-haired, with a patchy beard, was holding his nose and scowling at her. Gloria turned and ran—straight into the arms of yet a third man, older, heavier, and hairier. He picked her up by the shoulders and slammed her on the floor.

Alison admired herself in the mirror. The dress fitted her slim figure perfectly. She turned from side to

side, then tossed her head so her long brown hair swept
her shoulders and fell across the soft, smooth skin, right
to the edge of the neckline. *Lovely*, she thought. She
pulled up the skirt and admired the tiny stitching. The
seams were so carefully made that even if you wore it inside out, the dress would still look good. You didn't see
this kind of quality in Bornewald—they didn't have that
level of dressmaker here. She hadn't had a dress like it
since she was a child.

Come to think of it, she hadn't had a dress like this
even as a child. Her family was always too much in debt.
But she didn't care, she told herself, she really did have
a happy childhood. *You don't miss what you never had.*

Alison reflected on Gloria's scheme. She didn't think
much of it. It seemed silly and overly romantic—was all
that deception really necessary? In all honesty, she just
couldn't believe the king would fall for it. He wouldn't ac-
cuse her father of kidnapping. It was just too ridiculous.
And why was Gloria so intent on marrying some knight?
Oh sure, every girl daydreamed about a knight in shining
armor who would ride up and sweep her off her feet, but
when it came to brass tacks, was one boy really better than
another? They all seemed rather immature to Alison.

She pushed her hair back behind shoulders. She was
still facing the mirror, but her eyes were turned inward. *It
really would be nice*, she thought, *to go to the city.* To
visit the fine buildings and museums. To see a ballet and
an opera. To hang out with the princess and hobnob with
royalty. There would be lords and dukes and earls. They
would invite her to their balls and take her riding in their
carriages. There would be picnics in parks and parties on
patios. On the downside, the food in the city wasn't as

good as in the country. Their cooks had to use a lot of heavy sauces to disguise the flavor. Everyone knew that.

But she would be away from Count Bussard. "Damn that man. And the sorcerer who controls him like a puppet on a stick." Her father was right. It would be a relief to get away from this valley. She started to take off the dress, slipping the straps over her shoulders and pulling the bodice down over her breasts. Behind her the door opened.

She jumped and turned around, hastily pulling the dress back up. And then she froze, struck dumb, unable to move or speak.

Standing before her was the most beautiful man she had ever seen.

He was tall. He was slim, but she could see he had powerful arms. Long black hair curled around his neck in glossy waves. He was taking off a pair of stylish riding gloves. His black silk shirt was open at the chest, showing bulges of smooth muscle. His black calfskin belt was set off with a shining silver buckle, and his black cavalry boots were polished to a high gleam. At his waist was a court sword with a jeweled scabbard. He turned his gaze upon her, and their eyes not only met, the pupils shook hands, exchanged business cards, and sat down for tea together. He smiled at her, showing a firm jaw and even white teeth, and when he spoke, his voice was a rich, deep baritone that entered her ears and sent vibrations all down her spine.

"Come with me," he said, and held out his hand.

Entranced, Alison took it.

Terry attacked immediately. The sun had barely cracked the horizon when he and Roland left their horses

tethered to a tree by the side of the entrance road. He had
waited until he saw Roland tiptoe across the remains of
the rose garden—a patch of bare, thorny canes at this
time of year—and stealthily slip in through the unlocked
patio doors. Terry smiled to himself and jauntily circled
the manor house on foot. It looked to be the start of a fine,
clear, cold morning. The sun was shining, the love of his
life was waiting inside, and he even had a few coins in his
pocket. He resisted the urge to whistle. Turning a corner,
just outside the kitchen door, he saw two men tying a
heavy burlap sack across the front of a saddle. The man
in the saddle wore a sharply creased, gray-green uniform
with officer's markings. The two men on the ground wore
swords, breastplates and rough uniform-like clothing of
the same color. Terry didn't recognize the uniform, and
he didn't care. It wasn't the king's uniform. The men
didn't look reputable, and the screaming voice from the
kicking mass inside the sack was undoubtedly Gloria. He
drew his sword and charged.

Can one man with a sword defend himself against two
armed opponents? The answer is yes. It has been done
before, many times. If the swordsman has his back to a
wall, or even better, if he is in a doorway, so that he is defending a narrow front, forcing his opponents to face his
sword, then one man can fend off the attacks of several.
There are well-documented instances of fast, skilled
swordsmen holding off a half dozen enemies.

Ah, but can one man with a sword successfully *attack*
two well-armed men? Terry had heard that it could be
done. He had even trained on the technique. Conventional wisdom was that you had to rapidly switch your
blows from one opponent to the other, keeping them both

on the defensive, so that they didn't get a chance to coordinate a counterattack. He'd been told that if a man was very fast, and very skilled, and more than a little lucky, he could survive a fight under such conditions for two, perhaps three, minutes.

The officer saw Terry first. He shouted something, and spurred his horse. It disappeared around the corner, carrying Gloria with it. The two other men had their swords out in an instant. Terry struck the first man with the full force of his charge. The kidnapper blocked Terry's sword, but fell backward. Terry had no time to finish him off, though. He whirled and parried a thrust from the second man, made a counterthrust, which was blocked, and whirled again to attack the first man. And so it went.

The men were not bad swordsman. If Terry had a fleeting thought that this might be part of Gloria's plan, it was quickly dispelled. They wielded their blades with professional competence. But they were wary of this strange attacker, and had no experience of fighting in tandem. Terry managed to hold his own, striking at one and then the other, always staying in motion, always forcing them to keep their guard up. But he knew that it wasn't enough. He couldn't fight these men to the finish. He had to rescue Gloria, and the kidnapper on the horse was escaping.

So having started the fight, he now tried to break out of it. That was a mistake. It encouraged his two opponents, who thought he was trying to flee. They closed in, and now Terry was on the defensive. He parried strike after strike, with no chance for a thrust of his own. The three swords clattered like rain on a tin roof. His back was to the manor wall, and he quickly maneuvered himself into the doorway.

But the two henchman apparently knew this trick.
The younger one broke off the fight and disappeared
from Terry's sight. The other one, older than Terry, and a
skilled, experienced swordsman, kept up a careful attack.
Terry was getting winded. It was obvious what they had
in mind. The second man would come through the front
door and attack from behind. So Terry let himself get
pushed back through the kitchen. The next room was the
dining room. In an instant he clambered backward across
the table, putting it between himself and his opponent.
"Roland," he yelled. "A little help here!"

The henchman broke off the fight and stood back. He
kept his sword at high guard, and his eyes were narrow.
He clearly was wondering if Terry was trying to bluff
him. He angled his body cautiously and let his eyes flick
toward the dining room entrance, too quickly for Terry to
make a move. Both men quietly circled the table, each
waiting for his chance if the other man dropped his
guard. "Roland!" Terry called again. And his opponent
ran away.

Once again Terry was the pursuer. The henchman
darted through the dining room door, with the knight
right behind. He chased the henchman through the house
and out the front door. They ran up the front drive. Terry
was faster. He almost had him. He could hear the henchman gasping for breath. He was only a sword's length
away. One thrust through the kidneys, and it would be
over. But Terry couldn't risk it. He had to take the man
alive, to make him tell where Gloria was. He strained for
an extra ounce of speed, enough to get his hands on the
henchman's belt. And then the other thug ran Terry down.

The younger thug had retrieved their horses. Riding

one and leading the other, he rode into Terry at full gallop. Terry was knocked to the ground. He dropped his sword to protect his head with his arms, and curled up into a ball to avoid the pounding hooves. The two horses galloped over him, steel shoes ringing on the paving stones, only inches from his chest. He rolled away unharmed, saw his sword lying at arm's length, and reached for it. Before he could rise the first thug kicked him in the head.

And then kicked him a second time. Terry didn't lose consciousness—at least he thought he didn't—but it was a long time before he was finally able to stand again. The three men, their horses, and the princess, were long gone. He leaned on his sword for support. His face was wet. He touched a lump on his forehead, looked at his fingers, and realized that blood was running down his face. The ringing in his ears slowly subsided. He became aware of the silence. Not a sound came from the manor house. Outside, the birds had stopped singing, and the insects were quiet. The wind had died down. No breeze rustled the trees. Still in a daze, he looked at the empty lawn, crossed with long shadows from the morning sun, the quiet garden, and the blankly staring windows of the silent house.

"What the hell is going on?" he said out loud. And went back inside the manor.

Roland thought he was a very fortunate man indeed. Everything about the princess was delightful— her face, her clothes, her manner. He had already known that she would be beautiful. That was to be expected. A princess in the Twenty Kingdoms was always beautiful.

Some magical reason, no doubt. But he never suspected that she would be so charming. She sat across the table with her pretty face cupped in her hands and watched him while he talked. She looked absolutely adorable.

As he spoke to her, he made a mental note to thank the family for arranging his marriage. He was embarrassed at the way he had misjudged them. He understood now why they had put so much effort and spent so much money to get him betrothed to this girl. They obviously had his best interests at heart all along. His father especially. Who would have thought the old man had so much on the ball?

"More coffee?" he said out loud. She nodded, and he motioned for the waitress to refill their cups. The young waitress gave the princess a curious look each time she passed by the table, but said nothing. The princess didn't talk much either, not at first, and initially this bothered Roland. She had followed him out of the kidnappers' lair without saying a word. She had remained silent when he put her on the front of his saddle and galloped back to the inn. When he spoke to her she just sort of looked at him in a dazed way, as though she were mute. Roland was afraid the kidnappers might have mistreated her. He had heard stories about kidnap victims who had become withdrawn, or even catatonic.

But once they reached the safety of the inn, she brightened up considerably. This reassured him. He ordered coffee for them both, and the inn's whole range of cakes and pastries, then babbled on about the weather, the fashions in the city, art, theatre, wine, anything to distract her from her ordeal. Her expression now seemed to be one of adoration, although he couldn't think why. *She's probably just grateful to be safely away from that place*, he thought. It wasn't until he made a comment on the baked goods that she finally spoke to him.

"The Westfield Bakeries are the best in Medulla," he declaimed. "I will go so far as to say that we have the finest bakeries in the Twenty Kingdoms. We use only - top-quality ingredients, and all our bakers are carefully trained. We designed the ovens ourselves, and each one is custom-built to exact specifications." He picked up a wedge of jam torte and examined it critically. "Yet I have to admit that this little country inn has outdone us in certain respects."

The girl tilted her head a little. "You think so?"

"Oh yes. Take this torte, for example. Most places put in too much sugar, hoping the extra sweetness will overwhelm the palate and cover up deficiencies in the crust. But when you get a filling like this, only semisweet, that's a sign that the cook knows what she's about."

The girl's lips curved into a warm smile. "I've often thought the same thing. How nice to hear an independent confirmation."

Roland couldn't help expanding a little. "I dined here last night. The rolls they gave me at dinner were truly excellent. Light and fluffy on the inside, delicate and crispy on the outside. Trust me, when it comes to baked goods, I know what I'm talking about. It's not easy to get a good rise from your yeast on these cold, damp days. Even worse for baking is a gusty wind, when the draught from the stove varies and makes it difficult to maintain an even temperature. I'd like to meet the cook here. Maybe learn some of her techniques."

"I expect that could be arranged," said the girl.

Roland felt as though he could talk to this girl all day,

and the next day, and the day after that. So many women
talked of nothing but clothes, but this princess knew how
to keep up a conversation. Nonetheless, he was starting to
get a little worried about Terry. The knight had made it
clear to Roland that they weren't to wait on each other.
Whoever found the Princess first was to take her straight
back to Medulla. "If you're captured, sit tight, and eventually your family will pay the ransom, or I'll come back
and get you out. We're not in the same sort of danger a
girl is. If I'm captured, don't worry about it. Just bring the
princess back to her family. I'm not worth any ransom,
and I can defend myself."

Roland thought this was rather noble of Terry, but he
waited anyway. The bandits didn't seem to be pursuing
them, so he didn't feel under pressure to escape. And he
feared the princess might not yet be strong enough to
handle a long, hard ride. All in all, it just didn't seem
right to ride off and leave Terry behind.

So he was quite relieved when Terry burst in the front
door. The relief turned to concern when he saw that the
knight had a bloody cloth wrapped around his head. The
concern grew when Terry ran to his table, and shouted,
"Princess Gloria has been kidnapped!"

A bad blow to the head, thought Roland. "Yes, Terry.
Calm down. Sit down. Let's take a look at you."

"She's gone!" shouted Terry. "They carried her off!
I was right there! I couldn't stop them!"

"No one is blaming you," said Roland soothingly. He
quickly looked through all the windows, in case the brigands had followed Terry to the inn. It seemed quiet
enough outside. "It's all right now. Just sit down. Hold
still while we get this cut cleaned up."

Terry sat down, then stood up immediately. "We can't wait. They're getting away. We have to go after her now!"

"Not to worry," said Roland. "The princess is right here." He pointed to a chair and noticed that the girl he had rescued was not in it. Confused, he looked around and saw her coming out of the kitchen with towels and a basin of water. "I mean she's right there. She's fine. There's nothing to worry about. Just relax and let us take care of you." He took the basin from the her and smiled gratefully. "Let's get that bandage off."

Terry knocked his hands away. "For God's sake, Roland. How can you hang about here footling with the hired help when the princess is in danger? We have a crisis, can't you see?"

"Terry," said Roland firmly. "I want you to sit down, and take some long deep breaths, and have some tea, perhaps with a spot of whiskey in it, I think. The Princess Gloria is not in any danger. She's right here. Take a good look at this girl. Don't you recognize her?"

"Of course I do! She's the cook at this inn."

Roland chuckled. "No, she's the . . ." He stopped when he saw the expression change on the girl's face. "Aren't you?"

"No," said Alison. "I mean, yes. I mean, I do cook here." To cover her confusion, she dipped a towel in the basin and started washing Terry's head.

"What were you doing at that manor house?"

"Um," said Alison. She remembered that both the princess and her father had told her to distance herself from the kidnapping. "I was bringing food to the Baron." That was true, pretty much.

"They have takcout in a town this size?"

"We just started offering it."

Roland's dreams of marital bliss were crushed, the fragments now blowing away like dried leaves in a winter wind. Not wanting to let go of his fantasy, he said, "But you're awfully well dressed for a cook. Correct me if I'm wrong, but isn't that dress by Aubergé on Couture Street?"

"Um," said Alison. "The princess gave it to me."

"It's pretty common for ladies to give their old clothing to the servants," said Terry. He got up from the table and started pacing around the room.

"Oh. Right," said Roland. "Yes. Well, that explains the shoes."

Alison looked down at her shoes and opened her mouth to speak, but Terry cut her off. "Will you forget about this girl and get your stuff, Roland? We need to get moving. We need to find Gloria."

"You're not going anywhere right now." Roland pointed out the window. "Your horse is winded and exhausted. It needs to rest, and frankly, so do you. I'll tell the stable to take care of your horse. You go upstairs and lie down."

"We don't have time," said Terry frantically. "Every minute she is getting farther and farther away."

"So you'll track them again. Come now, this shouldn't come as a surprise. It's not uncommon for kidnappers to change locations, to move their hostage from one hideout to another. I was expecting something like this."

Terry looked stricken. "Oh my God." He put his hands in his hair.

Roland clapped him on the back. "You tracked them here even when they had two days' head start. You can certainly track them now with two hours' head start. Buck up. I have faith in you."

"I . . . I'm not sure I can track them." Terry swallowed hard. "Roland, you see . . ."

"The first thing to do is get back to the manor and talk to this Baron Wayless. He's obviously in cahoots with the brigands."

"Is the Baron all right?" Alison tried to keep the anxiety out of her voice.

"He was fine when I left him," said Terry. "Maybe a little shook up."

"He'll be more than a little shook up if he doesn't cooperate with us," said Roland grimly. "Normally I don't condone the use of strong-arm tactics on witnesses. But in a situation like this, they are justified."

"Wait a minute," said Alison. "What did these men look like? Did you get a good look at them?"

"Professionals," said Terry. "Gray uniforms. But not military, nothing I recognized. More like some local militia or some lord's private guards. Not your average thugs. Too good with the swords."

"Gray uniforms with red epaulettes and shoulder bars? Black leather buttons?"

"Yes."

Alison nodded. "You don't need to question the Baron. I know where they're going. I can take you there."

Lieutenant Scorn was not a good-natured man even in the best of times, but today's ride from the Baron's manor to Count Bussard's castle exacerbated his ill temper. He had expected the girl to calm down after a while, or at least tire herself out, but she had kept struggling the whole of the long hard gallop. When he got to the castle he simply let her fall off the horse onto the ground, then picked up the sack, carried it inside, shoved it into a closet, and locked the door. All this was done without seeing another person—the maids were not allowed in this section of the castle. He went back to his office, where he found a clothes brush to knock the road dust off his uniform and a towel to wipe off his boots. Then he went into the guards' mess room and drew a mug of beer.

He had hardly sat down when Thursby came in. The young guard threw the Lieutenant a salute. The Lieutenant threw one back, and said sourly, "Took you goddamn long enough to get here."

"We weren't expecting armed bodyguards, sir. There were at least half a dozen of them, maybe more. They seemed to come out of nowhere. Gave us a hell of a fight, sir. We beat them back and got away, but it was near thing."

"There was only one guard. I expected the two of you to make short work of him."

Thursby looked reproachful. "It saddens me to have my word doubted like that, Lieutenant. It denotes a lack of trust between an officer and the men he commands. If you refuse to accept my report of the situation, it will only . . ."

"I was there."

"Oh. Right. Well, he was big enough for two men. And he fought like six."

"Where the hell is Muchluck?"

"Don't know. He was right behind me, then I looked for him, and he was gone."

"He's right here." Muchluck dropped a handful of scraps on the table. The older and heavier of the two guards picked his own mug off the counter and filled it without waiting for the Lieutenant to return his salute.

The Lieutenant leaned forward. "What's this?"

"Lace."

"I can see that it is lace, Muchluck. Are you going to explain yourself fully, or are you expecting me to play twenty questions with you?"

"Came off the girl's dress. She dropped them to leave a trail. I picked them up. That's what took me so long."

"Muchluck, I don't know where this stuff came from, but that girl did not drop anything. She's tied up, she's inside a sack, and the sack is tied shut. She is not capable of dropping trail markers."

Muchluck shrugged. "Whatever you say, Lieutenant"

Scorn glared at him. Muchluck affected not to notice. He set his beer down on a bench, sat himself down beside it, took out his sword, and began wiping it down with an oily rag. Thursby, following his example, did the same thing with both his beer and his sword. The Lieutenant watched them until his own mug was empty. Then he made an impatient sound, pushed his chair back, and went to check on the prisoner.

He waited outside the door for a minute, listening for sounds of movement, before he unlocked it and entered the closet. It was really a storage room, about six feet by four feet. There were no windows. To his satisfaction the sack was not moving. The top was still tied shut. It lay in a hump where he had left it. His suspicions were allayed but did not disappear entirely. Remaining inside the closet, he opened the door and shut it again.

Immediately the sack started moving. Enough light came in under the door to see a slim, pale hand wiggle its way through the small loop of opening in the top of sack. The hand was holding a brass lace pin. The Lieutenant watched in near disbelief as the girl in the sack, showing a truly astonishing amount of dexterity, used the pin to pull apart the knot. The sack opened and a blond head, holding a very angry expression, emerged and looked at him.

Furious, Scorn walked out, slammed the door shut, turned the key in the lock, and stomped back to the mess room. "What the hell did you do back there?" he yelled at Thursby and Muchluck. "You damned idiots grabbed the wrong girl."

Thursby looked at Muchluck, who calmly sipped from his mug. "We didn't get the wrong girl, Lieutenant. We've been scouting the place out for the last month. He's got one daughter. There are no female servants. He doesn't get visitors. That's her."

"The Baron's daughter has long brown hair. That girl is blond."

Muchluck shrugged. "So she changed it. Women are always doing stuff to their hair. Sometimes you can't hardly recognize them."

"Don't jerk me around, Muchluck. I don't know who you've got in there, but you damn well better get the Baron's daughter over here before the Count finds out you've screwed up."

Thursby look anxious. Muchluck set his mug down, stood up, buttoned his jacket, and finger combed his hair. He walked past the Lieutenant without looking at him. After a moment, the Lieutenant got up and followed him. Thursby made up a third.

They caught up with Muchluck just as he was unlocking the closet. Gloria was completely out of the sack now, but the closet wasn't heated, and she had pulled the burlap over her legs for warmth. She was seated against the wall with a tatting spool in her hand. She looked up sullenly. Three men were standing outside the closet door, examining her minutely. Muchluck swept off his hat and bowed from the waist. "Excuse me, miss. I'm very sorry to disturb you, but we could not help remarking on the loveliness of your hair. Would you mind telling me if you've changed your color recently?" He gave her his best smile.

The question was so unexpected that Gloria, caught off guard, automatically smiled back. "Why yes. Do you like it? I originally planned to go with Soft Summer Peach, but then I thought no, that's a bit too brassy, so I decided on . . ."

Her answer was cut off when the Lieutenant reached past Muchluck and slammed the door shut again. He locked it and pocketed the key. "All right, it's her. Keep watch on this door until the Count is ready for her."

It was, in fact, several hours before Count Bussard was ready for her, although Gloria did not spend all that time in the closet. Lieutenant Scorn came for her after an hour, grabbed her arm with unnecessary force, and took her upstairs to small alcove with a glassed-in balcony. The room was unheated, but despite the cold, had a table that was set for lunch. A stack of envelopes lay by the single place setting. The Count had been preparing to read his mail. Gloria waited until the Lieutenant left, locking her in, and looked carefully through the glass. They faced the castle's rear grounds, allowing a fine view of fields and forest. A sheer drop prevented escape through the windows.

She shrugged, helped herself to fruit and finger sandwiches, and settled into the chair with the latest broadsheet, brought from the city by special courier.

Count Bussard entered an hour after that, stopped in his tracks, and stared. He was a heavyset man, not exactly fat yet, but starting to show jowls and the beginnings of a double chin. He was of late middle age, old enough for his hair to be completely gray but not yet old enough to stoop. Apparently he was also not the sort to stand on formality, for the first words he spoke to her were, "Who the hell are you?"

Gloria did not answer. She made a gesture to indicate her mouth was full. She was about to speak when the Count turned away and slammed the door in her face, cutting off her words. By now, Gloria was getting used to slamming doors. She picked up the broadsheet again.

Bussard returned in a minute with Scorn. "Of course it's her," said the Lieutenant. "I was there, I supervised the job myself, I brought her back on my own horse. We were at the right place, she was the only girl there. She's the Baron's daughter."

"I gave you a complete description, you idiot. How could you get this wrong?"

"Yes, Sire, and she matches the description. Same age, height, weight, figure."

"The Baron's daughter has brown hair. Or don't you notice subtle little details like that? Long brown hair."

"Chestnut brown," Gloria contributed helpfully.

"Exactly. Chestnut brown they call it, or some damn thing like that."

"So she changed it. Come on, Sire, look at her. Anyone can see it's a cheap dye job."

"I beg your pardon . . ." Gloria began.

"All right now, young lady," interrupted the Count. "Who are you and what are you doing in Bornewald? The truth now. I have no time for games."

"I am the Princess Gloria of Medulla."

"Of course you are. And I am King Bruno of Omnia. I do not have the patience for this."

By this time it was becoming clear to the princess that Count Bussard was not the sharpest knife in the drawer. This did not surprise her. Many people are under the misapprehension that those who have amassed wealth or power must have some greater degree of intelligence or skill. Gloria knew many rich and powerful people and had learned that this was not the case. The smart people eventually learn that once you get beyond a certain degree of comfort, more money doesn't make you happier. They use the money they have to pursue other interests. The people who get really, really rich have no other interests. They are rarely clever, and often quite dull, but they devote all their time and energy to doing one thing. Such was the case with Count Bussard. He started out in life with a lot of property. He had set himself a goal of acquiring more—all the land in the Valley of Bornewald, and then beyond. He really wasn't very good at doing anything else.

In fact, it took Gloria a good half hour of explanations, answers to personal questions, descriptions of court life, and plain old name-dropping to convince Count Bussard that she was truly the Princess Gloria. Lieutenant Scorn was even more reluctant than the Count to accept the truth. "But she told me she dyed her hair blond," he said, after he and Bussard had left the room and locked the princess inside once more. "The Princess Gloria is already blond. Why would a blond girl dye her hair blond?"

"Because it's the kind of thing that women do." The Count was frantic. The fact that the Lieutenant disagreed with him convinced Bussard he was right. "Omigod, omigod, omigod. Do you realize the trouble we're in?"

"No, not really, Sire. You've been kidnapping girls for years."

"No one who counted! They were commoners! But kidnapping a princess of Medulla? King Galloway's daughter! It means the noose for us all."

"But we didn't kidnap her, my Lord. Well, I mean we did, but she was already kidnapped. Baron Wayless kidnapped her."

"Oh yes, I'm sure he'd be happy to testify in our defense. Who would have thought he'd try something that desperate? Kidnapping? And a princess? I didn't think he had the guts. Wait a minute, maybe he planned it this way. He must have suspected I'd try to get his daughter, and he pulled a switch. He set me up! I'll get him for this."

"We'll have to let her go, my Lord. Explain that it was a mistake. Apologize."

"After tying her up and stuffing her in a sack? I'm sure she'll be in a forgiving mood. Sorry, Princess, we didn't mean to kidnap you, we meant to kidnap your hostess. I don't think so. We'll have to get rid of her."

"You mean kill her."

"Yes, yes, kill her, damn it. Bury her in the forest. Or put her in a bag full of rocks and dump it in a lake. Whatever it takes. It's the safest way. The trail ends with Wayless. Even if they track her to Bornewald, Wayless will get the blame."

"Yes, Sire. No, wait. It won't work. People saw us arrive."

"She was in a sack. No one here knows who she is. No one would believe Wayless or his servants. And it doesn't matter, because no one from this valley will talk anyway. The Middle-Aged Man of the Mountains sees to that."

Scorn was silent, thinking. "What?" said the Count. Scorn remained silent. "Don't tell me someone else saw her?"

"There was a man," the Lieutenant reluctantly conceded. "Not from around here."

"Who was he?"

"I don't know, Sire. He was big. He fought well. A knight, the men think, judging by his style of fighting and the type of sword he carried."

"Merely a bodyguard. Wayless must have hired someone to protect his daughter."

"Perhaps, Sire. But if that is really the princess, and she really was kidnapped, the king would have sent knights out to track her down."

"You have a way of making me feel better, you know that, Scorn?" Count Bussard looked at the solid door that lay between him and Gloria and beat his fist against it in frustration. "All right then. Get my signaling mirror. Meet me on the roof. I'm going to summon the Middle-Aged Man of the Mountains."

Terry, Roland, and Alison tethered their horses to a tree, and stood on a wooded hill looking over Count Bussard's estate. To the front were orchards and nut trees, then a long expanse of lawn. To the rear was more lawn, then cultivated fields, now bare and fallow, a few ponds, and finally thick groves of trees. A carriage road, lined with holly, led to a cluster of buildings. A purist might have said that the manor house was not quite fortified enough to be called a castle, but it was a very secure house, and Terry was not an architectural purist. He was willing to call it a castle. It had stone walls. Thick, solid doors. Heavy shutters. Black iron railings. Little stickers on the windows announcing that the grounds were patrolled by security guards. It was not the house of a man who was merely concerned about burglars. It was the house of a man who had made a lot of enemies and knew it.

Alison could have just given them directions, but she insisted that she had to take them herself. She wasn't sure why she said this. She had a lot of reasons, but she was still trying to straighten them out in her mind.

Unlike Gloria, Alison did not have a plan. She did, however, recognize an opportunity when it came along. She hadn't really been comfortable with her father's idea. He didn't have long to live. They both had learned to accept that. But she wanted him to die peacefully in a comfortable bed, with her by his side, and some memorable epigram on his lips. Not dangle at the end of a rope. Now there was a chance that the blame for the kidnapping could be shifted to Count Bussard. Ha! There was a man whose death would solve a lot of problems. Not just for her, not just for her father, but for most of the people in the valley. If Alison was a witness, she could help swing the story her way.

That's what she told herself. But there was another reason. She just wanted to be close to Roland.

She still was trying to sort out the man in her mind. She had kept her horse close to his while they rode so she could chat with him. Unfortunately, this time around she found herself babbling to him instead of listening. She told him about the inn, and her cooking, and the other girls who worked there, and customers who came in from the valley, and how she thought the inn should be run. He seemed quite willing to listen to her talk, but it was like she couldn't control her tongue.

She tried to piece facts together. The princess was expecting to be rescued by her boyfriend. And here was a boy to rescue her, right on schedule. But the princess said she didn't want to marry her fiancé. And Roland seemed to be her fiancé. Something wasn't right there.

The princess said her boyfriend was a knight. Terry was a knight. Did Gloria say her boyfriend was named Terry? Alison frowned, trying to remember if the princess had ever actually said her boyfriend's name.

No, that wouldn't make sense. Her boyfriend and her fiancé wouldn't be working together. Anyway, she couldn't believe any girl would choose Sir Terry over Roland. Roland was much better-looking. And he was rich, well dressed, educated, dashing, and elegant. She didn't see why the princess objected to marrying him at all.

She mulled over the problem some more and decided she had it figured out. Somehow Gloria's boyfriend had been delayed. Roland and his companion in arms had beaten the boyfriend to the punch. Now they would rescue the princess, who would then have to marry Roland. That was too bad for Gloria, yet somehow Alison could not bring herself to feel sorry for the girl.

Roland was the first to speak. "What do you think?"

Terry had been silent the whole ride, and his face held a grim expression. He hadn't joined in the conversation between Roland and Alison. Now he answered, "He has his own guard. Not a huge number of them, but they are more than us, and they're competent. A full staff of servants. A smooth, well-tended lawn, with very little brush to hide behind. Dogs roaming the grounds. Barred windows on the first floor."

"Which means what?"

"It means it would take a small force of men, a score at least, to assault that castle. We're not going to force our way in by ourselves."

Roland nodded. "I'm thinking that our first course of action is alert the local sheriff, or whoever enforces the king's law around here."

"Bad news," said Alison. "Count Bussard is the local justice. He owns the law around here."

"But if the constabulary knew that he was holding the king's daughter prisoner? Would they support Count Bussard over the king?"

"The king is far away. The Middle-Aged Man of the Mountains is right on that peak." She aimed her hand at one of the mountains that guarded the pass into Bornewald Valley. Terry and Roland followed her line of sight, to a wicked-looking spire of rock that jutted above the surrounding hills like a shark's tooth. The sky had begun to cloud up, but they could locate the sorcerer's mountain fastness, which hugged the cliffs and no doubt had the kind of view that upscale hotels charge big money to see.

"Who?" Roland said.

"The Middle-Aged Man of the Mountains. Count Bussard is his running dog lackey."

"His what?"

"His agent. Bussard handles his local affairs. In exchange the Middle-Aged Man of the Mountains uses his abilities to squash anyone who defies the Count. He's just the sort of greedy imperialist fat cat . . ."

"This is news to me," interrupted Terry. "What happened to the Old Man of the Mountains?"

"He retired to Silver Oaks three years ago. The Middle-Aged Man of the Mountains took over the business."

"Huh," said Terry. "I've never heard of the Middle-Aged Man of the Mountains. But then, I didn't know very much about the Old Man of the Mountains either. No one did. Just that he was mysterious and very powerful."

"And very wealthy," added Roland. "We can be sure of that."

"Why? What do you know about him?"

"Silver Oaks is a very expensive retirement community. Thirty-six holes of golf."

Roland stopped talking when he realized that Terry wasn't listening. Instead, the knight looked Roland over with a thoughtful expression. Then he switched his gaze to Alison. Eventually his eyes returned to Roland. "I fought with two of his guards. They know what I look like."

"Yes?"

"But they haven't seen you."

"No."

Terry looked at Alison again. "You're uncommonly well-spoken for a girl of your status."

Alison kept her face expressionless. "Thank you, Sir Terry."

"And by good fortune, you're wearing a designer dress. Do you think you can pass yourself off as a gentle-woman for a short time?"

"I'm certain of it."

"That's our plan, then." Terry looked from Roland to Alison and back again. "The two of you are going to walk in the front door."

"What?" said Roland and Alison, which was the reaction Terry expected although he didn't think they would synchronize it quite so well.

"Yes. It's a natural. Young couple from the city, out seeing the countryside, staying in Bornewald for a few days. Naturally you'd pay a social call on the local gentry. Maybe you're even thinking of relocating here, buying some land, so naturally you'd want to speak to the Count."

Alison said, "Count Bussard would never release land here. He only wants more."

"They wouldn't know that until they spoke to the Count."

"Who will," said Roland, "immediately have us put in irons."

"No. There are two possibilities, Roland. The first is that he knows who you are, in which case he'll think you're too rich and well-connected to kill, um, at least not right away. What is more likely is that he won't know who you are, but you're obviously rich and well-connected, so he isn't going to do anything until he does learn who you are. Either way you're going to get in the door."

"I don't think he's going to be taking visitors, Terry. He's got a kidnapped girl in there."

"Yes, so he's got to act normally. He's going to do what everyone else does. Invite you in, offer you drinks, exchange pleasantries, even give you lunch if you hint you're hungry. And then boot you out again as quickly as decently possible."

"All right, Sir Terry," said Alison. "I agree that we might get inside." Alison knew full well that they would get inside. Bussard had been trying to kidnap her, after all. Getting out would be the problem. "If he doesn't invite us inside," she continued, "we'll simply be turned away with no harm done. But assume we'll be invited into his castle. Then what?"

"I'll attack the place," Terry said. "It will create a diversion. I'll draw off the guards, get the attention of the servants, and you, Roland, will have to find the princess and get her out of there. Yes," he continued, in response to their doubtful looks. "It's not much of plan, but it's the best I can think of. I'm open to suggestions if anyone has a better idea." In truth, Terry did not like his own idea at all. It meant that Roland, if he found Gloria, would get the credit for the rescue. Then his engagement to her would truly be unbreakable. But Terry couldn't think of anything else. This wasn't a game anymore. The plan had gone all wrong. They were in a real kidnapping now, with real danger, and his first priority was to return Gloria to safety.

"I'll need to wash up and reapply my makeup," said Alison. She pointed to a stream, not far off, that bisected the copse of trees. "Give me a few minutes, please."

"Wait," said Roland. He turned to Terry. "We can't do

it this way, Terry. I'll confront this Count and make an offer on some land, but we can't put this girl in harm's way."

"You haven't seen the princess," Terry reminded him. "And she has. We don't know what other girls might be inside."

"And I know some of the people in the Count's service," said Alison. "They may be willing to help me, but they are not likely to help a stranger. You know how insular small towns are."

"We won't need them," Roland told her confidently. "Sir Terry has informants in this area also."

"He does?"

"Ah, not exactly," said Terry.

"He can't talk about them, of course. But they keep him informed of suspicious activity throughout this valley."

"Um, sort of," said Terry. "But I didn't learn anything about Count Bussard."

"That's decided then," said Alison, before the two men could decide anything. "I'll just be a minute."

She lifted her shoulder bag and went off to freshen up. Roland watched her leave. "What a fine, spirited girl."

"Oh yes," said Terry. His instinct was to encourage Roland's interest in any girl who wasn't Gloria. "Lovely, bright, personable, a good head on her shoulders."

"Fun to talk to," said Roland. "Although you don't want to get her started on dialectical materialism."

"What?"

"I couldn't figure it out either. But a nice girl."

"Just your type, really. I think she likes you, too." Terry thought he detected a hint of wistfulness in Roland's gaze.

But Roland merely shrugged. "Then I'll have to be careful not to give her any encouragement. I have no objections to fraternizing with the working class, myself, but the family would not approve of her."

"You're rich enough. You can marry any girl you want. Your family will get over it."

"I don't have any money of my own. My family will cut me off if I don't marry the princess."

"Oh," said Terry, who understood Roland's situation quite well. "Money is always a barrier." It was odd how people looked at it. Of course you needed enough money to be comfortable, and you had to take care of your girlfriend's needs, but beyond that it just got weird. What if a seventy-year-old man married a seventeen-year-old girl? It happened sometimes, and then people told you how sorry they felt for her. They wondered what sort of hardship or desperation forced the poor girl to marry that lecherous old pervert. Unless the old man was seriously rich. Then perceptions changed. The girl was considered a gold-digging hussy who somehow tricked a befuddled old man into matrimony.

His reverie was interrupted by Roland's words. "Of course, if the sale of sliced bread continues to decline, we might all be working in kitchens ourselves."

"That bad, eh?"

"It's not a problem yet, but the trend is obvious. They would see it, too, if they'd open their eyes."

"Alison told me she was able to sell more sliced bread by toasting it."

"We tried that," said Roland dismissively. "You just end up with a slices of dried-out bread."

"Well, it was an idea." Terry watched Alison return

from the stream. It was odd. She had been in their sight the whole time and hadn't appeared to do much, but now her hair was brushed to a smooth luster, her makeup had been tastefully touched up, and her dress seemed to be fresher and smoother. Terry looked at Roland. The man's hair looked perfect. Terry realized that Roland's hair always looked perfect. Even when it was windblown it seemed to suit him. Terry had the feeling that in contrast to the two of them, he looked like someone who spent his nights sleeping on park benches.

He gave a mental shrug and turned to his horse. By the time Alison rejoined them, he had opened his pack and removed a small crossbow and some tools. Roland and Alison watched as he disconnected the shoulder stock and the stirrup, leaving behind a pistol grip. When he was through he had something that was short and compact and nasty-looking, in the way that a small growling terrier can look meaner and inspire more caution than a large hunting dog. He handed the remainder of the crossbow to Alison. "See if this will fit in your bag."

It did, just barely. Alison's shoulder sagged with the weight. Terry took it back out again. Veins popped out on his face and neck as he slowly cocked the bow. When he had the string locked down he took a steel-tipped quarrel from his pack and fitted it into place. Then he gave it back to Alison.

"Hold it here," he said, putting her small hands on it, "and the trigger is here. Use it to defend yourself if you need to. It's small, and it doesn't have a whole lot of power, but it will kill a man at close range and even punch through light armor."

"Right," said Alison.

"Remember, the heart is in the center of the torso. Not the left side of the chest, where we put our hands when we make a pledge, but right in the middle of the body."

"Got it, Sir Terry."

Terry looked at Roland. "Roland, have you ever used that sword?"

"I've taken lessons with it."

"I mean, in a real fight?"

"No."

"You've never fought a duel?"

"No. I entered a tournament once."

"How did you do?"

"I got fourteen."

Terry was impressed. "Really? You scored fourteen points?"

"No, I had to get fourteen stitches afterward."

"Okay. Just remember, the heart is in the center of . . ."

"Yes, I heard."

"Okay then." Terry mounted his horse. "Give me time to circle around and get into the woods on the other side of the house. Then ride up in plain sight. When I take on the guards, do whatever you can." He wheeled the horse around, then stopped after a few paces to look back over his shoulder at their concerned faces. "Look happy. You're two young people in love, remember."

"Right," Roland and Alison said together. They smiled at each other, then each became self-conscious and tried to pretend they were pretending. They watched Terry ride down the hill and take the road past the castle. They could still see him when he reached the woods, although he seemed to be out of sight of the castle windows. He left the road and disappeared into the woods. They could only assume he was circling back from there. Alison put a foot in the stirrup of her horse, but Roland stopped her from climbing on, with a hand on her shoulder.

"Alison," he said. "Sir Terry is a knight, and as a knight, he has a code of behavior, the code of chivalry. This requires him to show honor, respect, and gallantry to a lady."

"Of course."

"By that I mean a woman of noble birth. Knights, I regret to say, are at liberty to treat common women roughly, and I fear Sir Terry is doing so with you. This is a volatile situation. You do not have to come with me. In fact, you should not."

Alison took Roland's hand off her shoulder. She meant to drop it, but for some reason she could not explain, she found herself holding it tightly. "And you, Roland, consider yourself a gentleman?"

"Well, yes."

"And a true gentleman, I believe, treats every woman as though she were a lady?"

"That's the goal, yes."

Alison smiled at him. "I think that is very sweet of you, Roland." She let go of his hand and swung herself onto her horse. "But as a cook, I have to say that this decision has been hashed over enough. Let's get moving. If we delay too long, we could put Sir Terry in danger."

They rode out of the copse of trees, down the hill, intersected the road, and finally turned into the drive that led to Count Bussard's castle. The holly hedge ran about eight feet high, which helped to deflect the brisk wind that was blowing across the fields. The berries were already turning red with the cold weather.

"We need to smile," said Roland. He demonstrated what he hoped was a fond smile, although in the back of his mind he held the suspicion that he was grinning like a fool. "Smile and talk to each other. Couples don't stop talking to each other until they've been married for a few years. They run out of things to say, I guess."

Alison had no problem smiling back at Roland. "I was going to ask you something. How is it that you've never seen the princess? You're engaged to her, after all."

"It is an arranged marriage. All marriages at this level are arranged. My family hired a firm of solicitors to negotiate with the queen and her team. I'm not certain that any of our people actually met with the girl."

"Yes, but didn't you involve yourself? There must have been opportunities to get a look at her. Weren't you curious?"

"I was busy with my work." Roland shrugged. "I don't see that it makes a difference. It is a marriage of convenience, after all."

A marriage of convenience? Alison puzzled over this. How could any man marry a woman he'd never seen? Until he had seen her, how could he know if he was attracted to her? If he wasn't attracted to her, would he still be able to . . . to . . . oh! A great light finally dawned on her. *Oh my!* she thought.

She looked at Roland with new eyes. *Of course*, she mentally berated herself. *How could you be so dense? It's obvious. The coiffed hair, the foppish clothes.* (She forgot that only a few hours earlier she had considered his clothes to be deliciously stylish.) *The way he knows all about art and theatre. Theatre!* Alison kept the smile on her face, although her heart seemed to slow down, beating sluggishly, as though reluctant to keep going. Aloud, she said, "What were you saying about my shoes?"

"Pardon?"

"This morning. You made a comment on my shoes back at the inn."

Roland looked at her foot, visible in the stirrup. "Oh. I merely meant to say that they didn't coordinate well with that dress."

Well, that clinches it, Alison thought. *You really do need to get out of the country, my girl. Imagine losing your head over this kind of boy. Maybe the city will teach you a little sophistication.* She shook her head ruefully, thinking about Sir Terry, Roland's buff, muscular "traveling companion." That should have been a dead giveaway right there.

Well, it was nothing for her to be concerned about, she decided. It was a bit of a disappointment, she was willing to admit that, but Alison reminded herself that the man was engaged, after all. She certainly didn't care what his private life was like. Not at all. She wasn't the kind of woman who would steal another woman's fiancé. Of course not. She was only here out of her concern for the princess. The poor girl. No wonder she had gone through all that effort to not marry him. It all made sense now.

Alison felt a little better, thinking how fortunate she was not to be in an arranged marriage. She smiled at Roland and continued chatting until they reached the end of the drive. Roland continued right up to the front door, where a guard appeared, looked at them suspiciously, and placed himself solidly in the path of the horses. Before he could say anything Roland stopped his horse, slipped lightly to the ground, and handed his reins to the uniformed man. "Roland Westfield," he said smoothly, "here to pay a social call on Count Bussard. Hand me your reins, my dear," he said to Alison, not giving the man time to reply. He passed them also to the guard, telling him, "Keep our horses ready, thank you. We shan't be staying long, I don't expect." He switched his attention back to Alison. "Let me give you a hand there, darling."

He helped her down from the saddle and up the steps to the front door, all the while keeping up a line of idle chatter, talking over any attempt to interrupt, either by the first guard, another one who appeared, or the servant who answered the door, to whom he simply handed over his card, and said, "Roland Westfield of Solcus. Is Count Bussard in? We were in the neighborhood and should like so much to meet him. If it is convenient, of course. No trouble, I hope. We don't mind waiting." And then they were past the butler and into the front hall. "Do bring my wife a glass of wine, thank you. And one for me as well. That will be all."

And then, amazingly, they were not only in the house, they were alone in the drawing room, a rather nice place, with thick carpet, antique chairs, and a few pieces of tasteful sculpture scattered between the furniture. The floor-to-ceiling windows were draped in gray-green cloth, trimmed with red and black. It was the same color scheme as the guards' uniforms. Alison thought that the Count must have gone upon a foolish tack when he sent men dressed in his own colors to commit a crime. Perhaps he meant it as a threat, to demonstrate to the village once again that he would use violence against those who resisted him. Or perhaps he'd just been stupid. Roland stamped his foot, then moved a corner of the carpet with his toe. "Teak floors. Imported. Very nice." He looked at a painting. "That could be an authentic Allessandro, or perhaps one of his students. I can't tell from here."

Alison also looked around. "It might be best if you suppressed your instinct to redecorate just now. The stairs are just down the hall. There's no one watching us. Should we run up and look for her?"

"There are too many people in the house. They will be after us immediately. Let's stick to the plan. Wait until Terry makes his move. Perhaps he really will draw them off."

Alison nodded nervously. She knew that Count Bussard had really intended to kidnap her, for God only knew what nefarious purpose. She wondered if he knew yet that the girl his men had taken was a princess. All during the ride she had rather enjoyed the idea of throwing his plot back in his face, walking up to him with an armed man by her side and knight waiting in reserve, threatening to set the king's men on him if he didn't release Gloria. Ha! That would teach the Count a lesson about trying to mess with her. Except there were more guards than she expected—at least six in uniform, perhaps ten. And there were a lot of servants, and plenty of them seemed to be strong men. As she added them up in her head, it began to seem that she had done something gravely dangerous. Perhaps it was time to explain herself. "Roland. I have something to tell you. I think there is a very good chance that Count Bussard will recognize me."

Roland nodded. "I was thinking the same thing."

Few other remarks can derail a train of thought so quickly. "You were?"

"We assumed that the Count would not recognize a

cook from the local inn. It's unlikely that he stays there, or eats there. But any of the guards or staff might, and they would tell him when you came in."

"Ah, that wasn't quite what I meant."

"No need to worry about it now, darling." Roland's voice had become smooth again. She saw that a servant had entered with drinks on a tray. "We'll discuss it with Count Bussard when he comes in. And if I'm not mistaken, this is him now."

Bussard was wearing a thick tweed suit and heavy walking shoes. In earlier days he had enjoyed walking over a newly acquired parcel of land, enjoying the fresh country air, listening to the birds singing, knocking the heads off wildflowers with his stick, seeing the grainfields sway gently in the breeze, and gloating over the way he had swindled or strong-armed the previous owner into parting with it all. One by one, all the freeholders had been reduced to tenant farmers. He didn't walk as much now that he owned nearly the whole valley, but the habit of wearing heavy outdoor clothes stayed with him. Roland stepped forward with his hand outstretched. "Count Bussard? Roland Westfield. Good of you to make time for us."

The Count ignored him. He stopped and stared at Alison, and his response was to shout at her, "What the hell are you doing here?"

Damn, thought Roland. *He did recognize her. He knows she's a cook.*

I need a plan, decided Gloria. It didn't take her long to come up with one. Her first step was to grab a candleholder off the table, smash a pane out of one of the French doors leading to the balcony, and feel around the outside of the lock to see if there was a key, or perhaps an outside latch. There wasn't, of course. She was on the third floor. She could think of no reason why anyone would want to lock a balcony door from the outside. But she checked it anyway, because architects do many weird things, and she would have felt like a damn fool if she broke down the door only to find that she could have opened it with a key.

Okay, so the door to the outside was locked, and the door to the inside was also locked. She felt over the frames on both doors, and under the carpet in front of each, in case someone had hidden a spare key. She didn't find one, and didn't expect to, but, of course, she had to check first. *Fine*, she thought. *No surprises there.* She examined the hinges. Both doors had them on the inside— could she pry them out with a teaspoon? No, the pins were covered with decorative knobs that needed a special tool to remove. Could she force the knobs off? Eventually, but she saw no need to be subtle. There was a quicker way. She looked at the table.

She carefully set the teapot, one cup, and a plate of finger sandwiches on the floor, in a corner of the room. She then flipped off the tablecloth, watching with no small amount of satisfaction as the rest of the Count's expensive china hit the floor. The carpet prevented it from shattering, but there were enough chips, cracks, and broken handles to make the set useless. Beneath the cloth, the table was made of ornately wrought iron, with a round marble top. It was heavy. Very heavy. It was perfect.

It was so heavy she had to crouch beneath it and put one shoulder under the edge to tip it over. It went over with a resounding thunk. Chips of marble flew off the edge. She hesitated a bit, listening carefully at the door, wondering if the noise had attracted attention. No one came in. So now all she had to do was roll the table against the door. Once, and the door bent. Most of the glass panes cracked. Twice, three times, and the wood frame splintered around the lock. The glass shattered and fell out with little tinkly sounds. Once, twice more, and the table broke through the door.

Cold wind whipped the curtains when she pulled the door back and stepped through. She found herself standing on a narrow balcony with a railing of wrought iron, facing a long stretch of open lawn. Behind it lay cultivated fields, now brown, with the remains of the harvest left on them, and beyond those a dark wall of forest. She nodded. That was her goal. If she could get to the trees, she could hide. She looked down, careful not to show too much of her head. She was on the third floor. Too high to jump. It wouldn't be a fatal fall, but she'd certainly break a leg or ankle, or even a couple of each. There were a lot of people below, standing guard, working, or going in and out of the building. It didn't seem possible to get across the lawn and the fields without being seen.

No matter. Terry would rescue her. He would come out of the forest on a charging stallion, his armor gleaming, his sword held high. He would sweep away any opposition, take her in his arms, and carry her to safety. He might even have a white horse. They were very popular with guys in the knighthood game.

She told herself that she wasn't just indulging in a

schoolgirl fantasy. She was a damsel in distress. Terry was a knight. He did this sort of thing all the time. Except for weekends. He liked to take those off, but he'd probably make an exception for her. Right this very minute he could be on his way to rescue her. He knew she was in Bornewald. He'd find Baron Wayless. He'd find her. She was sure of it. All she had to do was get down to him.

She stepped back inside and pulled the doors closed, bunching up the curtains to block the broken panes. From the corner she retrieved a cup of tea, which she sipped while eyeing the curtains and tapping her foot thoughtfully. No, they wouldn't do. Too thin, too sheer. Not strong enough.

That left the tablecloth. She set her tea aside while she examined it. It wasn't large, a square piece of natural cream linen with a Colmcille knotted pattern. While it was thicker than the curtains, it still wasn't particularly strong. But she decided that three strips braided together ought to make a rope that could hold her weight. She could then tie the braided pieces together. Although braiding would make the pieces shorter, she estimated she could get twelve feet of rope. Allowing a foot to tie off to the balcony, and if she climbed down and hung from her fingertips, she would drop—hmm—about ten feet. Yes, ten feet should be safe enough, even on hard ground.

She opened her knitting bag, extracted a pair of embroidery scissors, and got to work cutting the tablecloth into strips. This took quite a while, as the tiny scissors were not made for this job. After that the braiding went fairly quickly, but she had no idea how much time had passed. There was no clock in the room, and the sky had clouded up, concealing the sun. *I have to hurry*, she thought. *Terry will be here soon.* She didn't know how he would find her, but she was certain he would. Perhaps he would even find the trail of lace that she had left. In the back of her mind, doubts about this tried to surface. She ruthlessly pushed them back down. Of course he'd rescue her.

She finished the rope about the same time she finished the sandwiches and tea. She tested it by tying one end to the hall door handle and leaning back on it with all her strength. Satisfied that it would hold her weight, she untied it from the hall door, eased the balcony doors open, crept outside, tied off one end of the makeshift rope to the iron railing, and sneaked a look over the top. And there he was.

Yes! She congratulated herself. Did she have perfect timing or what? She stood up and waved her arms. Terry was streaking across the brown fields on a fast horse, sword held back and low, his other hand wrapped in the reins and guiding the horse carefully. He came to an irrigation ditch and jumped it smoothly, without even jerking his sword, and then came to a low stone wall separating the fields from the lawn and jumped that. A hole opened up in the clouds, long enough to briefly bathe him in sunlight. Gloria thought he had never looked so dashing. She made a mental note that when she got home she would commission an artist to paint this scene.

By now Terry had attracted the attention of Count Bussard's small force of guards, who were riding out in a jagged line. Terry swept his sword forward as the first one met him, and the wind carried the clashing of swords to Gloria. She was a little surprised to hear that the swords actually rang when they clashed, not musically like church bells but a clanging sound like cowbells. The blow unseated the guard from his horse, tumbling him off onto the damp grass. Terry didn't slow down. He parried a blow from another guard and rode right through the line, straight for the castle. The guards turned their horses around and followed him.

Gloria waved her arms some more. "Terry! I'm over here!" He apparently didn't see her. He reached the castle doors, where more men on foot were running out with staves and pikes. Terry rode past and slashed the air in front of them. They drew back. The horsemen behind him closed in. The knight turned his steed parallel to the castle walls and rode directly under Gloria's balcony. She could look right down at him. Her homemade rope nearly brushed his head. He still didn't see her. "Terry! Up here!" Her words were drowned by the thunder of hooves from the pursuing guards. Terry rode around a corner of the castle, disappearing from her sight. The guards followed him. All was silent.

Gloria ran inside and threw her weight on one set of white chiffon curtains. The curtain rods tore out of the wall and came down on her. She carried the curtains onto the balcony, held the curtain rod at one end, and waved the cloth like a big white banner. But her grip wasn't strong enough, and a sudden strong gust of wind took them away from her, blowing them across the lawn. "Damn." She ran back and got the other set, holding them more tightly this time. The cloth billowed out from the walls of the castle, like a flag indicating surrender or a really big sale on wedding veils. Either way it was impossible to miss.

But he did miss it. The thunder of hooves announced that the riders were coming back around the other side of the castle. Terry appeared first, leaning low over his horse's neck. His sword was in its sheath. The guards were in a tight pack now, close behind him and getting closer. Gloria hung over the railing and waved the banner frantically. "Over here, Terry!" But he didn't even look up. To Gloria's shock, he spurred his horse and turned it back toward the woods. A few minutes later he vanished into the maze of black trunks. The gray guards disappeared with him. Gloria was left with only the cold wind for company.

She let the chiffon banner slip from her grasp. "He left me," she said unbelievingly. "He ran away and left me." For a long time she stood dully at the balcony rail, staring at the distant woods but not seeing them, her thoughts turned inward. She didn't even notice the fluttering of wings over her head, or the black shadow that suddenly enveloped her.

The manor was in turmoil, but it was organized turmoil. Scorn, in a remarkably short time, got his guards together, while also assembling a cadre of footmen and stableboys to get them armed, armored, and mounted. Muchluck was standing at a first-floor window, watching them ride out with an ornate brass spyglass, when Bussard hurried past. "You two!" the Count said, stopping and pointing a finger. "What are you standing around here for? Don't you realize we're under attack! Scorn said he wanted every man out there!"

Thursby shifted his feet uncertainly. He looked to

Muchluck for guidance. Muchluck spoke without taking his eye from the spyglass. "Yes, Sire. The lieutenant gave us his orders."

"Then why are you standing—where did you get that spyglass?"

"From your desk, Sire."

"Give that to me!" Bussard snatched it out of his grip.

"We're not under attack, Sire," Muchluck continued. "One man is not an attack. It's that same knight who was at the Baron's manor."

"A knight? A knight of the realm! My God, one of the king's men?" Bussard fumbled with the spyglass, trying to capture the action outside.

"They hire themselves out for private work, Sire," explained Thursby. "We think that's what happened here. We can't think of any reason why the king would send a knight to Bornewald. You keep it all nice and quiet." He took Muchluck's place at the window. "Huh. The Lieutenant is almost on him."

"Yes," said Bussard. "I mean, no. I mean yes, there's no reason why the king would be angry with me. None at all. He has no reason to send a knight. What's he doing here?"

"Diversion," said Muchluck. "That guy is a pro. He isn't really going to attack a building like this single-handedly. He's trying to draw off our men while someone else sneaks in from the side. That's why Thursby and I decided to stay back."

"He's down!" said Thursby. "The Lieutenant is down!"

"Injured?"

"No." Thursby said resignedly. "He's getting up again."

"We'll check all the doors. And, Sire? Tell the servants

to latch and shutter the windows. That won't keep anyone out for long, but we'll hear them breaking in."

"There are already a couple of kids in here."

"What! I mean, I beg your pardon, Sire?"

"Alison Wayless and her boyfriend. They showed up here only half an hour ago. After all that trouble we went through trying to grab her, she knocked on the front door."

Muchluck had already been moving toward the drawing room. He stopped dead. "Sire? You let the Baron's daughter come inside? Then who is the girl that we brought to you this morning?"

"No one! Just some girl who happened to be hanging about the Wayless manor. She's nobody."

"But a nobody that the king sent a knight to protect."

"Nonsense! We don't know that. It's just a coincidence."

"And the Wayless girl, who hates you, shows up with some strange guy, and you let him in, too."

"I was trying to act normal."

Had Count Bussard not been of higher social class, Muchluck would have given him a withering look. Instead he tugged on his sword belt and asked, "Is the boyfriend armed?"

"He has a court sword."

Muchluck turned and walked away so fast the Count had to run to keep up. "Thursby and I will take that away from him. While we're doing that, Count Bussard, I suggest that you detain the girl."

"Agreed." The Count reached the door to the drawing room. He paused while he allowed Thursby to open it for him. Before he could turn the knob, Muchluck put a hand

on his shoulder and gently drew Thursby aside, then bent
low and put his eye to the keyhole. Not seeing anything,
he silently motioned for Thursby to pull the door open.
With his sword drawn, Muchluck went in first. Thursby
was right behind him. The Count followed them both.
Roland and Alison were nowhere to be seen.

The moment a charging, sword-waving knight
appeared out of the woods, there was a great rush to the
back of the house. The Count, the guards, and the servants sped to the doors and windows. There was a good
deal of shouting orders, slamming doors, and stamping
hooves, with plenty enough hustle and bustle to leave
Roland and Alison alone and temporarily forgotten. It
happened exactly as Terry planned it, something none of
them had really expected. Roland had to remark on it. "I
don't think I've ever seen a plan work so well," he said,
looking around the empty drawing room. "It seemed so
unlikely when he described it."

"The plan also called for us to find Gloria," said Alison. "We'd better start looking. They'll come back for
us pretty quickly."

"Upstairs, then."

It was a mystery to Roland why Count Bussard, or anyone else for that matter, would require a 147-room house,
especially as a good many of the rooms were to quarter
the numerous servants required to maintain the other
rooms. It proved to be quite impossible to search in any
reasonable amount of time. They trotted up the grand
staircase to the second floor, looked both ways, and arbi-
trarily chose to search the east wing first. Roland drew

his sword. Alison dug the crossbow out of her shoulder bag. At first they crept along on tiptoe, stealthily trying doors. Rooms opened into other rooms. They also had to open large cupboards and wardrobes in case Gloria had been stashed inside. A good many doors were locked. After they searched a half dozen unlocked suites they gave up all attempts at stealthiness and simply flung doors open, glanced inside, and raced to the next one. Finally, Roland said, "This is taking too much time." He found a bellpull and rang for a servant. "I suggest there is a simpler way."

It took less than a minute for a maid to appear, although to Alison it seemed an eternity. She was a very young woman who, judging from the looks she kept casting toward the windows, was much more interested in the spectacle outside than service upstairs. No doubt it was her lack of seniority that caused her to be sent to answer the bell when everyone else was watching the action. "Sir?" she said.

"Pardon me, my dear girl," said Roland. "Did you happen to notice if the Count has another guest staying with him? A young woman, medium height, fair-haired, well dressed, bound and gagged in a sack?"

"No!" said the girl instantly. Her eyes went wide with fright. "I didn't see her at all. Nobody noticed a thing! We were all busy elsewhere when they brought her in, so we don't know anything about it. Especially me. I don't know who she is or where she is and . . . and . . . that's not real, is it?"

"It certainly is," said Roland. He had produced a gold coin and was rolling it between his fingers. "And it's all for you, if you'll just lead us to her."

The girl's eyes fixed on the coin like a robin tracking a worm. Gold has that effect on some people. "I can't, I can't," she whispered. "The Middle-Aged Man of the Mountains. We dare not anger him."

"He'll never know about it." Roland had no idea what she was talking about. "He's out of town this week, attending a convention of sorcerers in Angostura." He put the coin in her hand. Her fingers automatically closed around it. "There you go. Just show me the way, then you can be off."

"Take us to her," said Alison "Don't waste our time."

Something about hearing the order from a woman in a designer dress seemed to reassure the girl. They were nearly at one end of the second floor of the house. She led them down the hall in the opposite direction from where they had been searching, to the west wing of the castle, where she opened a door to a short side corridor. At the far end was a stairwell. "She's up there," said the maid.

"Ah, this the service stairs, correct?" said Roland, looking up the dim shaft. "I'd really prefer it if you could show us . . ."

"Just go," said Alison, giving him a little push. "I'll stay here and guard the door." She hefted the crossbow.

"You don't need me, miss," said the girl. "Go up the stairs, and she's in the room at the end of the hall on the left. I have to go." She pushed past Alison and ran away, the gold coin clutched tightly in her fist.

Alison looked after her until the maid turned a corner. She switched her view to the grand staircase in the center of the castle, where she saw shadows moving. She pulled her head back inside and closed the door. "Someone else is coming," she whispered. "Quick, go." Roland hurried up the service stairs. Alison pressed her ear to the closed door, listening for footsteps, hoping they would pass by. The thick door and carpeted floor prevented her from hearing anything—there are times when quality construction is a drawback. She looked for the keyhole, but this door did not have a lock. Nothing happened for several minutes. She reflected that there were a lot of rooms to search. It might be a while before they got to this one. The temptation to take a peek outside got the better of her. She put down the crossbow, pressed her eye to the crack in the door, and gently turned the knob. She was about to pull the door open a bit when she felt the knob move under her hand. Hastily she jumped back and scrabbled for the crossbow. She just got it into position when Count Bussard entered.

"All right, that's enough of that, young lady," he said when he saw the crossbow. "Give that to me." He held out his hand.

This was a clear invitation to make a sarcastic remark before shooting him between the eyes. Alison refrained from doing either. She merely raised the crossbow and aimed it. This was not due to a gentle, spiritual, pacifistic nature, nor was she feeling an ethical dilemma that prevented solving problems through the use of violence. However, possession of a single-shot weapon pretty much forces you to only use it as a last resort. Once you've shot your bolt, so to speak, there's really not much else you can do except stand around and make small talk. Nonetheless, the rage that she felt whenever she thought of Bussard bubbled up from inside her. It must have shown clearly on her face, for Bussard raised his hands defensively and took a step back.

"What the hell did you think you were doing, Count Bussard, trying to kidnap me? You selfish idiot! Did you think Papa was going to sign over his land as some sort of ransom? Because that's just crazy. Contracts signed under duress aren't valid."

Bussard lowered his hands. "Thank you for that unnecessary legal assessment, Alison. Please try to remember that I am the Justice of the Peace here. A contract is as valid as I say it is. However, I had something a bit more subtle in mind for you."

The girl's finger tightened on the trigger of the crossbow. "I have something a good deal less subtle for you." For a moment Alison forgot all about Roland and Gloria. She thought instead of the families that had been ruined by Bussard, and her own father driven to bankruptcy. Her hands were shaking, which made the crossbow no less threatening. Bussard jumped backward and slammed the door.

He spent a long minute motionless and silent, for there is something about staring at the point of a loaded crossbow that makes the heart beat faster, and not from affection. When he turned around, he saw that Muchluck and Thursby had been standing behind them. "She's in there," he said, gesturing at the door.

"We saw," said Muchluck.

"Go get her."

"Sure," said Thursby.

"Of course," said Muchluck. Neither man made any attempt to move.

"Oh, come on," said Bussard. "She's just one girl."

"With a crossbow."

"She's only got one shot. There are two of you."

"What a totally convincing argument," said Much-luck.

"I've always been inspired by your leadership, Sire," Thursby added. "If you wouldn't mind disarming her yourself, just this once, I'm sure I could absorb the technique."

"Goddammit! I'm giving you an order!"

"Uh-huh. Count Bussard," Muchluck began to explain, "you know how it is in the dispatches when there's a big battle and some officer orders one of his men to do something totally stupid? And because of—I don't know—loyalty or dedication or something, the guy goes and does it? Well, this isn't one of those times."

The Count's face turned red with fury. Just as quickly he calmed down when he saw someone new approach them from the grand staircase. It was Lieutenant Scorn, walking with the stiffness of a man whose back has recently absorbed the impact of a heavy fall. He had already brushed most of the loose mud from his clothes, although they were still stained, and now he was attempting to clean his hands with a handkerchief. "He unhorsed me," he told the Count. "But the rest of the men drove him off. We'll catch him and bring him back. I suggest you give him to the Middle-Aged Man of the Mountains, along with the girl. Why are you two still here?" he demanded of Muchluck and Thursby.

The two guards saluted him, apparently just to see him wince slightly from his bruised shoulder as he returned the salute. "Your men believe that this knight has companions who infiltrated the house," said the Count.

Scorn gave them a disparaging look. "I find that unlikely," he said. "There was only one man, and we chased him off. I'm talking about our guards who are actually out there, following their orders," he said pointedly to Muchluck and Thursby. "Nonetheless, since you two suggested it, you can look for them. I want the house searched, room by room. Start downstairs and work up. Get on with it."

"Quite right, Lieutenant. We will all search," said Bussard. "We were doing that, in fact, when you arrived." He slapped his pockets, then gestured at the door. "Lieutenant, I believe I dropped my snuffbox in the hall there. Would you be so good as to retrieve it for me?"

Scorn gave him a curious look, then opened the door. The Count, Muchluck, and Thursby all stepped to one side as he entered. They heard the *twung* of a bowstring, followed by the *thunk* of a falling body.

Bussard turned to the two guards. "Now go in there and get her."

Roland found the door that the maid had indi-cated. It was heavy, it was secure, and it was locked. He'd have to come up with something heavy to break it down or something long and stiff to pry it open. First he had to know if it was the right door. He knocked on it gently, softly calling, "Princess? Princess Gloria?" There was no response. He repeated the knock and call again, both louder this time. Still no response. He decided to bring up Alison and have her guard the door, while he searched for tools.

He went back down the hallway, down the side stairs, and found the Alison trying to whack Count Bussard over the head with the crossbow. One of the Count's uniformed guards was trying to restrain her. Bussard had both arms in the air to ward off the blows.

None of the three noticed Roland until they heard the rasp as he drew his sword. "Let her go."

Thursby didn't have his sword drawn, and both of his hands were full of struggling girl. He yanked Alison around so that her body was between him and the point of Roland's sword. "Drop it, kid, or I'll break her pretty little neck."

"I don't think so. Let her go, or I'll run my blade through the Count here."

"Give her to me," said Bussard.

"Don't think so," said Thursby, not taking his eyes off Roland.

Roland saw his calculating look and interpreted it correctly. "Forget it. You'll have to let her go to draw your sword, and I'll run you through before you can get it out. If you don't let her go, I'll kill the Count here. You've only got one hostage, and there are two of you."

"I can do the math," said Thursby.

"I could swear I've had this conversation before," said Bussard. "He's an amateur with an ornamental sword, Thursby. Give the girl to me and kill this idiot." His confident tone was belied by the fact that he was edging around behind Thursby while he spoke. "Ow!" he finished, as Alison kicked him in the ankle.

"You know, Sire, you've got a point," said Thursby. He suddenly swung around and shoved Alison into Bussard's arms. Then he faced Roland, arms akimbo, hand away from his sword, and said, "All right, come and get me."

Roland hesitated. It was a mistake, but it was understandable. The guard in front of him was defenseless, and the Count was struggling with Alison. He should have just lunged immediately, but he suspected something was wrong. He was right. Just when he made up his mind to attack, he felt the point of a sword prick his back.

"Okay, kid," said a voice behind him. "Now drop it." It was Muchluck, who had run up the main staircase to the third floor, and back down the service stairs, to cover Roland from behind.

Roland gritted his teeth, but dropped his sword and raised his hands. Thursby drew his own sword and stepped forward to collect Roland's. Alison momentarily stopped struggling. Bussard grabbed a handful of her hair and turned her head around.

"So much for that," he said to her. "I had the notion of keeping you here in my castle, but now I don't think I'll bother. The Baron's line ends tonight." When she tried to kick him again he twisted her arm and bent her head forward.

"Let her go, Count Bussard," said Roland. "She had nothing to do with this. Your evil plan for the princess will never work. The king will . . ."

"Oh shut up," the Count told him. He let go of Alison's head. Keeping a tight grip on her arm with one hand, he drew Roland's visiting card from his pocket and waved it in the air. "Roland Westfield? Of Westfield Bakeries? And you dare to call *me* evil? You sell sliced bread! Little children eat that stuff."

"That's hardly a fair comparison . . ."

"Bring them to the roof and chain them up," Bussard ordered the two guards. "You know what to do. We'll leave them for the Middle-Aged Man of the Mountains. By morning our problem will be gone." He pushed past them and went up the side stairs, apparently either not sharing Roland's reluctance to use a servants' entrance or simply finding it more discreet not to lead prisoners at sword point through the middle of the house.

Roland clenched his fists. Muchluck saw this movement and jabbed him again. "The first one of you who tries anything, we'll kill the other one." He looked at Thursby holding Roland's sword, with its jeweled hilt, and took a good look at the scabbard buckled around Roland's waist. It was edged in silver and held a few jewels also. Muchluck removed it, while carefully keeping his eyes and sword point on Roland. "Now move along."

Roland reluctantly followed the Count to the third floor, followed by Muchluck, followed by Alison, followed by Thursby, who was now carrying two swords, the crossbow, and Alison's handbag. They turned a few corners, until Bussard stopped at a narrow door. Unlike the rest of the castle doors, which had crystal knobs and sported contrasting paint and trim, this was painted plain white, with a simple black iron bolt and no other trim. The Count put his hand on the knob. He tossed a key to Muchluck. "Get the other girl and bring them all up. I'll go out and watch for him. When we see him coming, we'll leave them there and withdraw to safety."

The guards nodded and marched Roland and Alison to the end of the hall. Muchluck ordered them to stand with their hands against the wall, then stood guard behind them while he let Thursby unlock the door. The two guards fumbled around a bit with keys and swords and handbags—Thursby was reluctant to hand over the jeweled sword to accept the key—but eventually got into position to grab Gloria if she tried to run away. Roland

noted it was indeed the same door he had knocked on—
the maid had not lied to him. Such is the power of gold.
"Don't move," Muchluck warned him again. But even if
he had a plan, Roland had no time to act on it. For
Thursby unlocked the door.

The handle twisted out of his fingers like a coiled
snake. The door was flung open and a fist shot out and
punched Thursby square in the middle of the face.
Thursby fell on his back with a thump. Terry came out of
the room with a leap like a mountain stag. He kicked
Thursby in the head and turned around quickly enough to
parry a thrust from Muchluck. It was the only thrust the
guard got a chance to make. Roland tackled him from behind. They both went down to the floor. Terry kicked
away Muchluck's sword and put his point to the guard's
neck. Roland got up, took his own sword and scabbard
back, and buckled it on, while Alison stooped and grabbed
Thursby's sword. Thursby sat up and put his hands to the
sides of his head.

There followed a long period of panting while everyone got their breath back.

"Are you two okay?" said Terry. "Did you find Gloria?"

"No, Sir Terry." said Alison. "How did you get here?
What happened to the other guards?"

"I drew them off into the woods, lost them there, and
doubled back. They'll be back soon, though. Where is the
princess?"

"We thought she was in there with you."

Terry shook his head. "No. I saw her on the balcony
when I rode past, but when I came back she wasn't there.
She waved a banner to signal me, though. And she left a
rope for me to climb up. That helped me get in."

Roland pointed at the open door. "The count said she was in there. And one of the maids told us the same thing."

"Well, she isn't." Terry looked down at Muchluck, who was spread-eagled on the floor. He lifted the point of his sword a little bit so Muchluck could shake his head.

"The count also told us she was in there."

"Maybe she escaped on her own," said Alison. "Went down the rope and ran off while the guards were chasing you."

"No," said Terry. "There was a fight on that balcony, some sort of struggle. I've seen enough fight scenes to recognize one." He pointed through the open door. "She used the table to break down the windows herself, but then she fought with someone outside." He looked at Muchluck again. "Where is the count?"

It took another prod with the sword for Muchluck to answer. "He's on the roof. He is expecting us to bring her up."

"Let's go."

Back down the hall they all went, this time the two guards being prodded along by the three rescuers, until they came to the door where they had left Count Bussard. It was unbolted and open, and it contained yet another set of stairs, apparently leading to the roof. They were wide enough for one person, while maybe a second could squeeze by if they both turned sideways. Terry looked up. It was a steep flight, with another door at the top. The door was cracked open—he could see a bit of light alongside it. He turned to Muchluck. "Is that door made of iron?"

"The count had it reinforced after he started meeting with the Middle-Aged Man of the Mountains."

"What's up there?"

Muchluck and Thursby exchanged glances. "I'm not sure," Muchluck said. "Something bad. The Middle-Aged Man of the Mountains doesn't like strangers. If anyone ever went up there with the Count, it was always the Lieutenant."

"Right." Terry looked up the stairway again. "Well, now is your chance to satisfy your curiosity, because you two are going up first. Don't get any great ideas, like thinking you can dash through the door and slam it behind you. We're not stupid."

"Dashing onto the roof," said Muchluck, "and especially closing the door behind me, is the farthest thing from my mind."

They went up the stairs in a line. Muchluck leaned ever so gently against the door and tried to peer through the crack. He put his ear to the metal and listened. Finally he rapped on the metal, two soft taps. He said, "Count Bussard?"

From the other side of the door came a great flapping sound, a long whoosh and flutter, as if of huge wings.

"Run," shouted Muchluck. He grabbed the handle and pulled the door shut. Outside they heard the vicious scraping of claws on metal. The handle turned under Muchluck's fingers. He grabbed it with both hands and leaned back, putting all his weight into keeping the iron door closed.

"Gloria!" shouted Terry. He charged up the stairs, knocked Thursby down, and climbed over him. He reached the top step, knocked Muchluck aside, turned the handle, and pushed on the door.

And hit the ground as Thursby pulled his feet out from

under him. Muchluck grabbed the handle and pulled on it again. "Are you crazy? Don't open the door!"

"Gloria is out there!"

"And we're in here, and that's where we're staying!"

Roland came to Terry's aid and tried to pull Thursby off him. Thursby kept his grip on Terry and tried to kick Roland down the stairs. He lost his balance and tumbled into Roland, taking Terry down with him. Alison ran back down as all three men tumbled their way to the bottom.

Terry dug his way out of the pile first and ran back up. By now the noise had stopped. Muchluck was sitting on the top stair. He moved aside to let Terry pass. Terry went through.

He found himself on the flat top of a mansard roof. A wooden platform had been built outside the door, reinforced with thick beams, as if to take a heavy weight. Some of the beams had eyebolts driven into them, and some of the bolts had chains and shackles attached. A cast-iron stand held a lamp and a signaling mirror.

The shackles were empty. The platform was empty. The roof was empty. Count Bussard was gone. Not completely gone. His head remained, but even that was in less-than-pristine condition. Of Gloria there was no sign.

For six hundred years every legal textbook in the Twenty Kingdoms has described the case of Sir David of the Five Dragons *vs.* The Kingdom of Lacunae, or Five Dragon Davey as he later came to be known, and even later than that, simply Five-DD. It happened that the Kingdom of Lacunae was involved in a civil war, with King Hansen (Hansen the Arrogant) battling his cousin

Allen (Al the Termagant). With the castle under siege by
termagantic forces, King Hansen sent his family, under
military escort, into hiding, to a mountain redoubt he
had secretly constructed for just such an eventuality. Sit-
uated in a narrow chasm, concealed in the side of a cliff,
strong and impregnable, it had waited for years, silent
and empty, for just such an emergency. Unfortunately,
during those long years, dragons had moved into the area.

According to legend, a single soldier escaped to tell
the tale. Torn and bleeding, he staggered into a remote
village and described how the entire party had been de-
voured by a colony of dragons, except for the Princess
Gina, who alone had made it to the safety of the redoubt.
He even told the tale in rhyme and died after gasping out
the final couplet. This was a fairy-tale kingdom, remember. Things like that happened.

By the time the story reached the royal palace, King
Allen was in power, Hansen and most of his court were
dead, and nobody left alive was quite sure where the hiding place had been, or even if it really existed. Nor was
anybody particular eager to find it. The war was over.
There was a lot of rebuilding, replanting, reconstruction,
and reconciliation going on. The new king wasn't eager
to have an heir to the throne around, stirring up trouble.
Besides, if the story was true, the girl was dead by now
anyway.

Or so everyone thought. Until the day that Sir David
was called to the palace. The new king was sitting behind
a desk piled with stationery. The people were now calling
him King Al the Usurper and he had just finished getting
his letterhead and business cards reprinted. "Davey," he
said. "You gotta find Princess Gina for me."

"Get outta here," said Sir David.

"No kidding, I mean it. There's always some trouble-maker out there wanting to start up another revolution. We can't let them have a legitimate heir. She'd make it too easy for them to rally support."

"She's dead, Al." Sir David and the king had fought side by side and this put them on a first-name basis. "It's been a year. Even if she made it to safety, she's bound to have starved to death by now."

"That's why you gotta bring back her bones. With this damn silly story going around that she survived, there'll be imposters popping up for the next fifty years, claiming to be the rightful heir. We have to positively identify her as dead."

Sir David frowned. "Can you do that with just bones?"

"She'll have jewelry and rings and things that can be used to identify her. She'll have the royal hairband."

"The what?"

"She had a solid gold hairband. She was a sorority girl."

Sir David looked doubtful. "I don't know, Al. She's guarded by a bunch of dragons, according to the story."

"Sure, but that's got to be an exaggeration. You know how dragons are. They're too mean to live with each other. There's probably only one dragon."

"Oh, thanks a lot."

"Tell you what, Davey," said King Al. "You bring Gina's corpse back, you can have the hairband."

It took two months for Sir David to locate the mountain redoubt—he traced it through construction records. From her vantage on the cliffs, Princess Gina saw him before he saw her. She had been living for fourteen months on rainwater and ravens she had snared with the yarn from her needlepoint bag. She immediately sprang into action. From her handbag she took the last of her carefully husbanded soap and cosmetics, so by the time the sun made its way into the chasm and backlit her with golden rays, her hair was clean and brushed, her lips and eyelashes were perfect, and from a distance she looked as beautiful as any other princess of the Twenty Kingdoms. Except that she was half-starved, but that was okay. The waif look was in that season. Sir David fell in love with her at first sight. No kidding, he really did. Don't be so cynical.

There only remained for Sir David to slay the five dragons that guarded the fortress, and here Gina had not been idle either. During the year she had carefully tracked their habits and located their hiding places, and by means of the mirror in her compact was able to signal this information to Sir David. It was still a tremendous feat of bravery and skill to slay the five dragons—to slay even one dragon of any kind is impressive—and Sir David well deserved the accolades that were given him, but nonetheless it was a team effort. And then the two rode back together, to the cheers and adulation of the entire country.

Except the king.

"For God's sake, Davey," he said. He put his head in his hands. "You weren't supposed to bring her back alive!"

"Couldn't be helped, Al."

"I was just about getting everyone back to working together. She's been here three days and already the court is splitting into Termagant and Arrogant factions again.

Why couldn't you have pushed her off a cliff or some-thing?"

"Wouldn't be chivalrous, Al."

The king snapped his fingers. "I got it, Davey. You marry her."

"What?"

"Yeah, it's great. You're a Termagant, she's an Arro-gant. Oh yeah. The two factions are unified by love, everyone's happy, the press is gonna love this." King Al stood up. "Sir David, for your bravery, gallantry, and all that stuff, I'm rewarding you with the hand of Princess Gina. What a story."

"I don't know, Al."

"What's the problem? You said you loved her."

"Oh sure. I do. But, you know, when I first saw her I was just an ordinary knight. Now that I'm a big hero, I've got babes lining up around the block to spend the night with me. This isn't a good time to get married."

But when the king gives a reward, a knight really can't turn it down. King Al called Princess Gina in for a secret meeting, where he generously offered to not execute her, and even to name her as his heir, provided she would not contest his right to the throne. He gave her a contract to sign. Princess Gina read it over carefully, took the pen he handed her, and stabbed him through the eyeball with it. He had killed her family, after all, and fourteen months of living on water and raw birds can make a girl a bit testy. Then she married Sir David, reunited the country, and they both lived happily ever after.

Of course, these days every one in the Twenty King-doms *thinks* she died of starvation back in the mountains. That's because they only know the story from the famous opera, *Princess Gina*—score by Antonio Rosinetti, libretto by Jake McGurk—where she expires in his arms after singing the haunting aria *"Perché Siete così Ritardati?"* (What Took You So Long?). But that's opera. Opera is supposed to end tragically. The truth is that they both lived happily ever after AND set a legal precedent. When a knight slays a dragon, he gets to marry the next available princess. Nothing to it.

"A gryphon," repeated Alison.

"A gryphon," said Muchluck again. "They're big." He spread his arms in a gesture meant to indicate bigness. "Big enough to carry off a horse. They're mean. And they eat girls. That was part of the deal that Count Bussard had with the Middle-Aged Man of the Mountains. Even a sorcerer needs to buy things and make investments. The Count was his local agent. He kept things quiet for Bussard and Bussard kept things legal for the wizard. Or at least made sure the law looked the other way."

"You've seen him?"

"The sorcerer? No. He likes to stay on the sidelines, so to speak. He uses go-betweens, like Count Bussard, to deal with the general public. The Old Man of the Mountains worked the same way."

"Except for the girls he kidnapped. I expect they saw him."

"Perhaps. You can't count on anything with a sorcerer."

They had all left the roof and gone back inside, downstairs to the Count's library. It was well designed, with lots of tall windows for natural light, club chairs, and glass-fronted barrister bookcases. Roland searched the shelves, while Muchluck and Alison stood at a window and looked up at the sorcerer's peak. His mountain redoubt was shrouded in clouds, but Alison had seen it many times before. She felt a sinister chill just thinking about Gloria being taken there.

She shuddered and lowered her gaze to ground level. Bussard's force of guards had ridden away. Everyone was leaving. The servants were streaming away, walking swiftly down the graveled drive, or just cutting across the meadows, their belongings hastily packed in whatever container was available. "They're going back to town."

"We shouldn't be here either. It's not safe. Who knows what the sorcerer is up to? We going to have the king coming after his daughter on one side, and the Middle-Aged Man of the Mountains on the other side, and we don't want to be caught in the middle."

Alison had told the two guards that they had kidnapped the Princess Gloria, daughter of the King of Medulla. It took a little time to convince them, but hostilities had ended. Muchluck and Thursby were now more than eager to be cooperative. They were also eager to get the hell out of the castle. Even though Muchluck gave the impression he'd like another chance to mix it up with Sir Terry, he was willing to let a rematch wait for another time.

They both started at the sound of breaking glass. Roland came away from the shelves with a pair of thick books under each arm. "I only found a few things." He put them on a table. "They were all shelved together, and that shelf was locked." Alison stood next to him while he opened the thickest book. Although all the books had been dusted regularly, this one still looked very old. The leather over the spine had peeled away from the binding, and the rest of the cover had a pattern of fine cracks. "The earliest reference is by Aristeas, in his epic poem the *Arimaspia*. He says they originate beyond the Issedones, and continually war with the Arismaspians for their gold, which they dig up out of the ground and hoard in their mountain fastness. Give me that book, please."

Alison handed him the next book on the stack, a copy of the *Indika*. This one seemed newer on the outside, but the paper inside was yellowed and brittle. It had probably been rebound. Roland opened it to a marked page. "Ketesias the Cnidian places them in Scythia. He says they are extremely vicious, giant four-footed birds with claws like a lion and a head like an eagle. They have black feathers except for a red breast."

"Well, if this man is correct," Alison said, indicating Muchluck, "they are not in Scythia or the Issedones. There is one right here in Medulla."

"The sorcerer could have brought it in. Or hatched it from an agate egg."

Thursby entered the library, lugging two heavy pigskin valises. He gave one to Muchluck. "The maids took off with the silver plate before I could get to it. His valet got his rings and gold shirt studs. Of course the silver spoons were the first to disappear. I got a bunch of the silver candlesticks, and a silver cow creamer. The other guys already emptied the cashbox."

"If you're intent on looting this place," said Roland, "the artwork here is worth far more than the silver." He pointed to the opposite wall, which held a painting of a young woman holding a glass with ice cubes. "That's

Madonna on the Rocks by Ambrosia Pesce. It will bring a good price at any auction."

"Bought with money torn from the starving mouths of the oppressed masses," said Alison.

"Too hard to fence," said Muchluck. He stroked his chin thoughtfully. "Go back to his bedroom and get his silk hose," he told Thursby. "They're easy to carry, easy to sell, and they'll will fetch a pretty penny. Silk shirts, too, if you can fit them in. Then let's get out of here."

"Right," said Thursby. He looked at the books on the table. "You told them about the gryphon?"

"I did."

"Did you tell them what they eat?

"Girls," said Alison.

"Virgins," said Thursby.

Alison clucked her tongue in exasperation. "Again with the virgin thing? What's the big deal about virginity? Dragons, unicorns, sorcerers, priests—are they all obsessed with virgins? Why isn't the sadder-but-wiser girl ever considered for their nefarious schemes?"

Muchluck gave the young woman a speculative look. "There must be something particularly valuable about virginity, since so many girls are so reluctant to give it up."

"Enough of that," objected Roland. "I will appreciate it if you will refrain for lowering the tone of the conversation."

"Boys can be virgins, too," continued Alison. "So how come evil sorcerers never try to kidnap them?"

"Girls are probably easier for him to catch than boys," explained Muchluck. "They can't see him. When a man gets to middle age, he becomes invisible to pretty girls."

"What?"

The library door opened and closed again as Terry came in. His mouth was set in a hard, straight line. Without saying anything, he looked around the room until he spotted a vase of flowers. He picked it up, threw the flowers on the floor, and splashed the water on his face. Crossing to a window, he dried his hands on the draperies while he looked grimly across the valley, to the steep peak that housed the Middle-Aged Man of the Mountains.

"Terry." Roland interrupted his thoughts. "Where have you been?"

"In the stable. I had to secure our horses. The guards took the Count's horses when they deserted."

"Damn," said Muchluck. "I didn't think of that. We'll have to walk."

"First you'll show me to the armory. I'll need a lance and a long sword. And an ax will be good also."

"Battle-ax or chopping ax?"

"Either one will do."

"What are you going to do?" asked Alison.

"We have to bring back soldiers," said Roland. "You can't attack the sorcerer alone. There must be a military outpost in the region."

"Not in this valley," said Muchluck. "The Count took care of security."

"How far away then? A day's ride? Two days'?"

"Too far," said Terry. "There's no time." He pointed out the window. "It's a four-hour ride to the base of that mountain. Half a day to scale the peak. I can reach the summit before dawn tomorrow. Animals in zoos are fed once a day. In the wild they might eat less often than that.

Assuming it ate Count Bussard today, and the beast feeds once a day, there's still a chance to save her."

"Save her how? These things are big, Terry. They fight dragons. Have you ever seen one? Do you even know what they look like?"

Terry glared at Roland, then crossed the room and pushed past him, over to the bookshelves. Scanning them only briefly, he selected one, put out a hand, and pulled down a thick handbook, which he brought back and laid in front of them. *Fielding's Guide to Birds, Butterflies, and Monstrosities.* Terry flipped through the index, then riffled through the book until he found the page he wanted. "Look at this," he said, handing it to Roland. "There it is."

The others crowded around Roland to look at the book. "I don't believe this," said Thursby. "It says the Gray Warbler is native to the woods of Medulla. I've lived here all my life, and I've never seen a gray warbler."

"Other page!" snapped Terry.

"Gryphon," read Roland. They all fell silent, looking at the illustration.

"Oh my," said Alison.

Any competent fashion designer will tell you that there are certain combinations that don't look good together and never will. Usually he is talking about patterns, but fabrics and textures are also included. Silk socks with a tweed suit, for example. Pearls and black leather. Fur and feathers. The illustration, which a snarling mass of fur, feathers, muscle, claws, and a sharp, dripping beak, was of a monster that blended frightening and hideous with tacky. It looked like something made by a creator with a demonic mind who also had bad taste.

Roland cleared his throat. "Terry," he said carefully. "I don't want to question your professional competence, but I think this may be a bit out of your league. We should send for that other guy."

"What other guy?"

"You know. The one who killed the dragon over in Oblongata. I can't remember his name."

"Huggins," said Alison. "Sir Huggins. I heard about him, too. Roland is right, Sir Terry. We need someone like that."

Terry glared at her. "Huggins didn't . . . he's not exactly . . . I don't think . . ."

"I'm sorry if I hurt your pride, Terry. You're very strong and very brave. But we really ought to call in someone who has experience."

"Huggins doesn't really have that much . . ."

Thursby read the caption. "The diet of the gryphon consists primarily of young virgins."

"Just show me to the damn armory!" shouted Terry

There was nothing frightening or intimidating about the lair of the Middle-Aged Man of the Mountains. At least, not from the outside. In fact, with its overhanging gables and rough lumber walls, it put Gloria more in mind of a holiday ski chalet than the fortress of an evil sorcerer. She was not in a holiday mood, though. She regained consciousness on a bank of wet snow, shivering and cold, in a small courtyard. Her last memory was of the gryphon dropping her from roof height. When she looked up it was still above her, four clawed feet gripping the rocks above the chalet, and she clambered backward, hands and ankles sinking into icy slush, to get away from its hostile glare. Pure instinct brought her to the warmth of a doorway. From her knees she reached up to grab the handle, crawled inside the door, closed and bolted it, and finally pulled herself to her feet, leaning against the frame while she looked around.

She was standing on a parquet floor that was badly in need of polishing. A few area rugs were scattered across it. They too were well-worn. There were windows, but they were misted over with condensation and didn't let in much light. At first she didn't see anyone else. The focal point of the room was an overstuffed reclining chair. Next to it was an end table, with a lamp. When she was sure she could stand again without support, she walked over and looked at it. The table also held an illustrated book of back exercises, a scattering of pillboxes, and several empty bottles of low-calorie beer. The walls had several racks of shelves, mostly filled with old high school sports trophies

The room had a fireplace, which became Gloria's next destination. A small wood fire was burning with a steady flame. She warmed her hands and front until she stopped shivering, then turned around and warmed her backside until the wet material of her dress started to steam. Meanwhile she tried to develop a plan. She didn't see the Middle-Aged Man of the Mountains until he spoke to her. This surprised her, because he was sitting in the inglenook right next to the fireplace. Yet somehow she had looked right past him.

He had her sewing bag open, with the contents spread across his lap. He examined a piece of lace, holding it so the firelight shone through it, and said, "Very nice."

"I made it myself," said Gloria. The words sounded id-
iotic to her own ears, but she had to say something while
she looked him over. He seemed to be in his midforties
and in good shape, but with a small paunch that he would
never be able to get rid of no matter how many stomach
crunches he did. His hair, gray at the temples, had been
artfully combed in a vain attempt to cover a bald spot the
size of her palm. He was wearing a cardigan sweater and
khaki pants with an elastic waist.

As she had finished her examination of him, and he
was apparently taking no further notice of her, Gloria
decided to take the initiative. "I am the Princess Gloria,
of Medulla, oldest daughter of . . ."

"I know very well who you are," said the Middle-Aged
Man of the Mountains. He carefully arranged the contents of her needlework bag on the hearth. Not until he
was finished did he finally look up. "And you know who
I am, so we can dispense with the formalities."

"Very well. I'll thank you to return my sewing bag,
then you can explain how I may leave this mountain. You
need not trouble yourself to accompany me, I will make
my own way. I need hardly add that you are in a great
deal of trouble, however allowance can be made for your
cooperation from now on, so if . . ."

"You are not going anywhere," said her host. "I have
a plan for you. You won't like your part in it, I fear, but
on the other hand the unpleasantness will be short-lived."

"Excuse me," said Gloria. "But exactly what part of 'I
am a princess' did you not understand? My father has a
rather large and well-equipped army, and if you harm me
you will draw the whole of it upon you."

"I have done my investigations, Princess. The king

does not know where you are. His knights are searching the western half of Medulla for you. I don't know why a princess should be in the Valley of Bornewald, but the trail, if you left one at all, ends at Count Bussard's castle. If he let any of his men know what was going on, they're hardly likely to report it to the authorities." He looked Gloria up and down. "Very nice. Five and a half feet tall, curly blond hair, blue eyes, fair-skinned with a mole on your . . ."

"That's a beauty mark," interrupted Gloria.

"But nonetheless extremely attractive."

"Thank you, it's kind of you to say so. Now if we are through with the exchange of compliments . . ."

"But a princess of the Twenty Kingdoms is always beautiful, isn't she? Always. Apparently there is something magical about a princess. Something in the blood, perhaps."

"Something in the blood?" repeated Gloria. She was quite sure she didn't like the way he said that. Her brow furrowed, then her face cleared as she beamed at the sorcerer. "Ah, I see. I'm afraid you misunderstood me. You think I'm a princess. Not at all. I meant to say that *my name* is Princess. No, I'm not royalty at all. I know it's a bit of an unusual name, but you see, my mother wanted a child and my father wanted a collie, so when I came along they named me . . ."

"Blood," said the Middle-Aged Man of the Mountains. "My gryphon needs a fair maiden to dine upon." He said this with complete matter-of-factness. To Gloria, a gruesome statement said so easily meant she was dealing with a lunatic. "They prefer live prey," he added.

By this time it had become abundantly clear to Gloria

that the middle-aged sorcerer was not about to let her walk away. She was not happy about the situation. To be rescued by a brave and daring knight had a certain romantic quality about it, but you didn't want to make a habit of it. Even the most gallant knight might feel you were abusing your position. She turned toward the fire and warmed her hands again, but this was only so she could look around the room, checking the exits and windows, to see if she could make a run for it. "Of course," she said, talking to keep the sorcerer distracted, and also to quell the fear in her stomach. "Live prey. A fair maiden and a virgin, too, no doubt. On the other hand, there are plenty of inexperienced boys around, and no shortage of plain women either, but you sorcerers never seem interested in them, which makes me suspect that you're really just indulging some inner kink, rather than trying to meet a genuine magical specification."

"It's a question of supply and demand, I think," said the sorcerer. "Young men are expendable. They have no value. We send them into battle and slaughter them by the thousands. And old women? No one cares about them either. It's kind of a relief when they're gone. But when a pretty girl disappears, she is missed. She leaves a hole in people's lives. That hole, I believe, is what fills with magic. Or perhaps the magic leaks out of the hole. I admit it's still a bit of a mystery."

"Yes, well your pet out there was willing to chow down on Count Bussard, who was neither fair nor female, so I suppose a gryphon's diet is not as restrictive as all that."

"That's the male. He prefers horses, actually. The female is below. She's not fully grown. She can't fly yet, that one. She's nothing but pinfeathers now. But you're correct.

The food supply is a problem. I've been trying to bring her to maturity, but I just can't seem to find the right girls."

"What a shame."

"The girls want you to think they're all purity and innocence, but the gryphons can tell. Rather interesting, that. Unicorns have the same ability. Anyway, it didn't used to be a problem, but kids today don't want to wait."

"Sure."

"I blame the parents. They're so busy with their careers they don't have time to teach their children good morals."

"Oh yes, the double standards are not what they used to be. I can tell you're a very moral person yourself, so that must really bother you."

"Well, it's not like I do this all the time. Two gryphons, that's all I want. A breeding pair."

Gloria sneaked a glance out the window. She couldn't see the gryphon, but she would never forget what it looked like. The thought that someone would actually want to breed these ghastly creatures was revolting.

She didn't say this. She said, "How nice. I'm sure they make a lovely couple. I can understand how you must be looking forward to the pitter-patter of little claws around the place—this place—whatever this place is, but—think carefully before you answer—have you considered getting a puppy instead?"

"I don't give a damn whether they produce young," said the Middle-Aged Man of the Mountains. He clasped his hands, as though he was about to rub his palms together, but caught himself in time and made a steeple of his fingers. "As long as they build a nest. It's the gold I want."

"Say again?" Gloria took a step back.

"Gold! Don't you understand gold! They line their nests with gold! They search the mountains for it and they find it—I don't know how—and they tear it out of the rocks with their claws, and they build nests in the crags and it's all gold! Pounds of it. Hundreds of pounds of it. Tons of it, even."

"Oh great. Great. That's just great. Of all the lunatic lunacies to be loony about, I have to get kidnapped by a guy with gold fever. Other girls get kidnapped by twisted psychopaths with deep, dark desires. At least they get to go down in history as the victim of some unusually grotesque murder, but me? Noooo. Of all the trivial, mundane, run-of-the-mill obsessions, gold fever has to be the most inane." Gloria was working herself into a fury now. She was kidnapped, wet, chilled, hungry, frightened and to top it off, she felt that she had been deeply insulted. "Gold. It's a useless yellow metal that's only good for pierced earrings. You can't even make a decent frying pan out of it. Yet the world is full of people who spend their lives fighting for it, scheming for it, hoarding it, and drooling over it. Tons of gold, eh? You moron."

"It's true!"

"Yeah, I'm sure it is. Gold fever. I know your type. Always on the lookout for the next big strike. You spent your youth diving for sunken treasure, didn't you? And sometime in your past you went prospecting in the mountains, right? Probably you had a partner, someone you eventually dry-gulched over some trivial vein of ore. I'll bet you've got a box of gold coins hidden somewhere. Every now and then you pour them on your bed and roll around on them and sleep with them. Or maybe you keep them under the floor, stashed beneath the hearthstone." Gloria kicked angrily at the hearth and, to her own surprise, felt a loose stone shift.

"Stay away from that!" The Middle-Aged Man of the Mountains was on his feet. Gloria could see that he was wearing sandals with socks. He grabbed her arm and yanked her away from the fireplace. "For over a decade I've been working on this. I had to offer huge rewards for the gryphon eggs. I brought myself to the edge of bankruptcy. Scores of men gave up their lives attempting to steal the agate eggs and collect those payments. I kept them warm and turned them and hatched them in secret. I raised the young myself, and you will never, never, have any idea how much newspaper you have to put down under a gryphon. Now my plans are coming to fruition and you, my dear, are part of the finish."

"Let go of me!" Gloria got an arm free and slapped the sorcerer in the face. He hardly seemed to feel it. He merely smacked her right back, a blow that made her head snap to one side. Then he threw her down in the middle of the floor and waved his hands.

In front of her eyes the parquet tiles folded down to reveal a trapdoor. She wondered if he did this magically, or if he had rigged it up with wires and pulleys and activated it with a hidden switch. An acrid smell wafted out, the smell of dung and urine, that told her some beast was living below. Raising herself to her knees, she cautiously moved her head until she could see over the edge of the hole. She saw only darkness.

"I think they're like mosquitoes," said the Middle-Aged Man of the Mountains conversationally.

Gloria looked up. "What?"

"They need the blood to breed. Like mosquitoes."

Gloria still looked blank. "Or I could be wrong," he continued cheerily. The sudden mood swing gave Gloria more evidence that the sorcerer was off his rocker. "Maybe they just get a craving for an innocent girl. Like pregnant women who crave pickles. But I don't think anyone has ever fed a princess to a gryphon. Dragons, yes, but not a gryphon. We might see spectacular results. I could write a paper on this."

Gloria looked at the door she had entered through. That door, she knew, led into a courtyard, and that courtyard was guarded by a gryphon. There was no escape that way. There was another door that led inside. She didn't know where it went, but she'd have to risk it. The sorcerer stood in her way. She would have to rush past him. She tensed her muscles to spring.

The Middle-Aged Man of the Mountains saw her. "None of that," he said, and jumped at her. He reached her in a split second and landed a kick in her side that made her curl up in pain. Then he placed his sandal firmly against her back and pushed her over the edge of the hole.

Under normal circumstances, he would have followed this with a short period of standing over the opening, hands on hips, looking down in fiendish triumph, a sadistic smile playing across his evil countenance, and that sort of thing, but this particular act of malice was accompanied by a vigorous display of jumping up and down and scuffling around the edge of the hole while screeching, "Ow, ow. Let go of my foot!"

Gloria had managed to grab his ankle with one hand. Her fingernails were digging into his skin, while her other hand was flailing around, trying to get a grip on the smooth wood floor. She got an arm over the edge of the hole and pulled herself up until her head emerged. The sorcerer kicked her in the head and stomped on her fingers. Gloria slipped back down. He used his free foot to stamp on her arm, until finally her grip broke and she fell. As she tumbled downward, a long, drawn-out scream of terror, "Aaaiiiieeeeeeee," emerged from the lightless shaft and gradually faded away.

The Middle-Aged Man of the Mountains looked down into the pit. "Now what was that all about?" he said irritably. "That was only a twelve-foot drop."

"Excuse me." Gloria's voice drifted upward. "I'm the victim here. I'll scream how I like, thank you very much."

From the darkness she heard a scraping sound. She pressed her back against the wall, trying to make herself as flat as possible, listening as hard as she could. The scraping noise sounded again, a little closer. This time she identified it as the sound of claws on stone, and large claws at that. "What is that?"

"The other gryphon," said the sorcerer above her. He pulled down his sock and searched his ankle for broken skin. Two large welts were beginning to form. "The female."

"Yes, I assumed it was the other gryphon," said Gloria. She closed her eyes and opened them again, hoping they would adjust to the darkness more quickly. "It was a rhetorical question. Did you give it a name? I'll bet you did." She peered into the gloom. She could hear it moving, but she couldn't see a thing. Talking kept her courage up. "I'll bet you talk to it, don't you? I'll bet you stand at its cage and throw it raw meat and say things like, 'Who's a pretty girl, hmmm? Who's a pretty girl? You are. Yes, you are.'"

That was almost exactly what the Middle-Aged Man of the Mountains did, but he wasn't going to admit that now. He tried desperately to think of an original and clever name for a gryphon so he could make a snappy reply. "Griff" was definitely out, and he thought about "Agatha" because the gryphon was hatched from an agate egg, but he didn't really like that name. He was still thinking about it as Gloria's voice grew higher and louder. "And you know what else? I'll bet you look like a total idiot when you're talking baby talk to your gryphon." The Middle-Aged Man of the Mountains looked around for something to drop on her. He was about to settle on an ashtray when he saw the piece of lace on the hearth.

He grabbed it and flung it into the hole. "Here. Make a funeral veil. Something appropriate to wear while you're waiting to die."

Gloria voice was faint. "I was saving this for the Autumn Ball."

"Hah. Well, you can just—" He was interrupted. Gloria gave a short, sharp scream.

Then there was nothing but silence.

The Middle-Aged Man of the Mountains looked thoughtful. He stared at the hole for several minutes before he waved his hands again. The trapdoor closed. The floor sealed up as though the Princess Gloria had never been there.

To reach the crag that held the sorcerer's head-quarters required no special climbing ability. A paved carriage road, narrow but well maintained, switchbacked up the side and went right to the top. Unfortunately, Terry reached it just as the last rays of the sun were retiring behind the mountains. He drew his horse up at the base and inspected the road. In the murky twilight, he could see that it climbed steeply, with one side against a wall of bare rock and the other against a sheer drop. Still, it was wide enough for men on horseback. Mist swirled around the peak. High above, he thought he could see a single light glowing in a window. But it might have been sunlight reflecting off the clouds. By the time Roland arrived, the sky was black. Alison, lagging a little behind, showed up a few minutes later.

"It's too dark to ride," Terry told them. "One missed step could send us right over the edge."

"Shall we walk, then?"

"I'll walk ahead with a lantern. You two will follow and lead the horses. It's a steep hike, so we'll use them to pack the weapons. I want to save my strength for battle."

"No hurry," said Roland. "You can rest for a bit. We have all night."

Even Alison, if he could have seen her in the darkness, looked shocked at Roland's callousness. Terry glared at him. "We don't have time to spare. We don't know what he's doing to Gloria. Every minute counts."

"Terry," said Roland patiently. "You will be of no use to the princess if you're dead. Do you honestly think you can fight this animal in the dark?"

There was the type of pause that is often described as pregnant. Roland waited. "No," Terry finally said. "But I'm not waiting for dawn."

"The moon will be up in a few hours," said Roland. He pointed skyward, to a spot where the faint glow of the

Milky Way penetrated through a gap in the cloud cover. "The sky looks like it is clearing. When the moon comes up, we might even have enough light to ride."

Terry hated to delay when Gloria was in danger. But Roland had a point. "All right, Roland. I'll wait two hours. If it hasn't cleared up by then, we'll walk."

"Right," said Roland. Alison concurred.

They withdrew half a mile, where the road that led into the mountains crossed a road that skirted the valley, and a pub sat where the roads crossed. The windows were shuttered, but a thin tendril of pale smoke streamed from the chimney, dispersed by the cold wind. Terry sent Roland and Alison inside while he pumped water for the horses. The pub was a tiny place, with a bar the width of the room and two small tables by the door, but the bar-keeper was able to supply them with bread, cheese, and smoked sausage to go with their hot cider. Roland took one of the tables. Terry came inside and pulled a chair over, but told Roland he was going to look at the horses again. It was obvious to Roland that the knight was simply too wound up to sit.

Alison took a chair across from Roland and untied her scarf, then took a brush from her handbag and ran it through her hair. He took a moment to look her over. She looked very good, considering the hardships of the day and the hours in the saddle. The evening gown, which seemed so delicate, had held up surprisingly well. Roland guessed that was a result of quality material and good workmanship. Her eyes were in shadow, but the candle-light threw highlights on her cheekbones. She put the brush down and pushed back the her jacket, letting her soft hair fall around her shoulders. When the cider came, she put her hands around the mug to warm them and gave Roland a tentative smile.

Roland sternly reminded himself that everyone looks good by candlelight.

Roland still wore the silk and silver he had put on that morning, but he had traded his dress jacket for a gabardine traveling coat. It was double-breasted, with deep outside pockets. From one of them he removed a book he had taken from the Count's library—*De Natura Animalium* by Aelian. He asked the barkeeper for an extra candle, and opened the book to a page he had marked earlier. "It says here," he told Alison, "that gryphons are inimical to both horses and men, but they will not fight with the elephant."

"Very wise," said Alison. "I never fight with elephants myself."

"It confirms that they dig gold and gemstones out of the mountains for their nests. But it doesn't say anything about their diet."

"Maybe you'd better let Sir Terry do the fighting."

"Impossible." Roland turned the pages of the book. "He won't be fighting only a monster. He'll be fighting both a monster and an evil sorcerer. That's more than any one man can handle. Damn, I should have hired those two soldiers to go with us. I didn't think of it."

"They didn't volunteer themselves, either. They seemed pretty fearful of the Middle-Aged Man of the Mountains."

"They are mercenaries. Enough money, and they might have changed their minds. Too late now, anyway. We'll have to do it ourselves. I wish that picture gave a better idea of the size. I'd like to know how big this thing is."

"Those soldiers said it was big enough to carry off a horse."

"Sure, but how big is that? Are we talking big enough to swoop down and snatch up a horse, or are we talking about big enough to grab a horse but barely being able to lift off with it?"

"You should probably avoid the monster," said Alison. "Let Sir Terry handle it." She was thinking out loud, not noticing if her words had any effect on Roland. "Because, you know, they're supposed to have a diet of virgins. But that doesn't necessarily mean female virgins."

Roland frowned. "I don't expect that to be a problem. Not to be indelicate, but I have been around the block a few times."

"Oh sure," said Alison. She had her mug up to her face, so she missed Roland's expression. Unaware that she was steering the conversational ship directly for the shoals, she went on blithely, "I just wonder if, from a monster or magician's point of view, it might not count. Even if the man thinks he's a stud. You know what I mean."

"I'm afraid I don't." Roland's voice took on a bit of an edge. "Why wouldn't it count?"

Alison suddenly awoke to the fact that her ship was on the rocks. The thing to do at that point would have been to abandon the subject, jump overboard, and swim for safer waters. She elected, futilely, to sail on through. "All I mean is that a boy might still be considered a virgin if he didn't do it with a girl."

Roland closed the book with a snap. "What," he said sharply, "are you implying?"

"Nothing!" Alison frantically tried to reverse course. "I'm sorry. I just thought that, you know."

"No! What are you talking about?"

"Well, I mean with the clothes and all. And your hair looks so nice. And all that talk about wine and art and fashion . . . just seemed a little . . . and that stuff about the theatre."

"I see," said Roland calmly. "I apologize for not sitting at the table in a torn undershirt and incessantly discussing sports." Then he lost his temper. "Damn it to hell! Can't a man dress with a little panache, or show a little sophistication, without people jumping to conclusions!"

"Sure, if he's Italian. But normally men don't do it."

The raised voices drew the attention of the barkeeper, who decided it was time to interrupt. He came over with a pitcher and refilled their mugs. "Can I get you anything else?" he said. He looked from Alison to Roland. "Perhaps a bottle of wine?"

"No," snapped Roland. "Give me beer. In a dirty glass. And some greasy fried food. No, make that a steak. In fact, just bring a slab of raw meat."

"I'm sorry, sir. I'm afraid I don't have . . ."

"No need for a knife and fork. I'll eat it with my hands. And then belch afterward!"

"All right!" shouted Alison. "I said I was sorry!"

They stared at each other across folded arms. The air around them seemed to have grown suddenly chilly. They realized together that this was not an illusion—Terry had returned and left the door open. "The moon is out." He looked grim. "The horses are ready. I'm going." He went back out.

Roland dropped some coins on the table and followed him. Alison shrugged on her jacket and followed Roland. Roland was surprised to see that Terry had all three horses saddled up and ready. He looked over his shoulder at Alison, then at Terry, and said, "Alison should wait for us here. There's no reason for her to come with us."

"Neither of you are coming with me. The moon is bright enough to ride by, so I don't need someone to lead the horse. I'm going up to slay the monster, kill the sorcerer, and rescue Princess Gloria. You two will ride to the nearest army post and alert the military. If I don't come back with the princess, they'll send a division up this mountain and wipe this fellow out once and for all."

"And if you do come back with the princess?"

"Once they know the princess is safe, I expect they'll send a division up this mountain and wipe this fellow out once and for all. It's time for the king to take control of this valley again."

"Then there is no hurry," said Roland. "If the people of this valley want the king's help, then one of them can call for it. So I'm coming with you."

"I don't need your help, Roland. Sorry, but that's the truth. This isn't the first slay-and-rescue mission I've done. What can you do? If you're trying to show how brave you are, you don't need to prove anything."

For the merest second, Roland's eyes flicked to Alison and back. "Maybe I do," he said under his breath.

"What?"

"I can watch your back," said Roland loudly. "I can do that. You don't know what you're going to find up there. Don't say I can't help—you know that isn't true—and don't argue with me. We're just wasting time."

"Fine," said Terry shortly. He turned his attention to Alison. "Then it's your job to summon help. There's an army outpost at . . ."

"No," said Alison. "I'm coming, too."

Roland objected. "We don't need . . ."

"Don't start with me!" yelled Alison.

Terry looked at Roland. "Don't start with her."

"Right," said Roland.

But their best laid plans went aglee and a haft. The road had bad spots, washed out or weakened by autumn storms, so that they did have to dismount and lead the horses, step by step across loose stones, and the temperamental moon went off to sulk behind a cloud for an hour or two, which also slowed them down. They were above the snow line, and had to be careful not to slip on ice or patches of slush. Dawn was breaking by the time they approached the summit. The peak had a broad, flat face, so there was a little bit of a yard in front of the chalet, enough to turn a carriage or exercise a horse. The night's wind had swept it clear of snow, but now the wind had died, and the sun was rising into a clear blue sky, presaging a fine autumn day. From the outside, the chalet looked warm and cheerful, a perfect place to spend a winter holiday, although it must be admitted that the large, winged monster perched on the rocks above it detracted from the pleasant atmosphere.

"It doesn't look like a sorcerer's castle," said Roland. "I was expecting something more sinister. You know, a round stone tower with single gleaming red window. This place makes me think of hot chocolate and gingerbread."

"Maybe this is just his vacation home," Terry said sourly.

They dismounted before they reached the summit, left

the horses on the road, and traveled the last switchback on foot, concealing themselves among boulders at the side of the road. They saw the gryphon at once, of course, and the gryphon saw them. It was still perched on a ledge above the chalet. Pebbles trickled down where its claws scored the rock. It fixed them with a malevolent stare and stretched its wings a few times, but otherwise it did not move. Terry, who had gone ahead, slipped back to join the other two. They had concealed themselves in the rocks that rimmed the summit, wedged into a narrow gap beneath two boulders. Terry knelt beside them.

"What do you think?" said Roland.

Terry was carrying a longsword and an ax. He said, "You know how it is when you look at a drawing of a cruel warrior, or a vicious animal, and you expect that the artist exaggerated a bit and made the thing look more dangerous than it really is? Or how when you're riding through a dark night, and your imagination tends to run away with you, and you sense evil in every shadow, but you know when you see things in the light of day, they won't look nearly so bad?"

"Yes."

"I'm not getting that feeling." He gave Roland the ax. "Stay close to Alison."

"Okay," said Roland. He was already pressed up against her, which in other circumstances would have been quite pleasant. He hefted the ax a few times and nodded. Terry went back down to get his horse. Alison had a crossbow again, this time a full-size one from Count Bussard's armory. Terry had cocked and loaded it for her. She rested it on a rock and sighted it on the gryphon. "I suppose it wouldn't do any good to offer it birdseed."

"I suppose we could sacrifice one of the horses if we had to lure it down."

They watched Terry come back up the road. Neither of them knew anything about jousting, but they both agreed that the knight appeared to know what he was doing. He rode back up at an impressive clip, considering the terrain he was on. He wore a breastplate, shoulder guards, and a helmet, with a sword at his belt, a shield on one arm, and a lance under the other. The armor was the largest they could find in Count Bussard's storeroom, but it was still a tight fit. He held the lance and shield just the way that knights always carried them in paintings Alison had seen, so it looked right to her. Roland also thought he seemed deadly enough. Perhaps the gryphon did, too, because it failed to attack.

It kept a wary eye on the knight, snarling at it and flexing its claws. Terry circled around, making jabbing motions with the lance, trying to goad it into an attack. Several times it opened its wings and flapped them, as though it was about to take off. But each time it settled back onto its perch. Perhaps it had had a bad experience with lances at one time, or perhaps it was trained only to attack on command. Perhaps it was just too early in the morning for it to fight. Whatever the reason, it stayed where it was.

Terry rode back to where Roland and Alison were sheltering. They stood up. "Okay," the knight said. "If we had the element of surprise working for us, we've lost it now. I don't like this. It smells like a trap. But we need to find the princess."

"Can you hold it off while we run inside?"

"That's exactly what I had in mind."

"Front door, do you think?"

Terry looked at the chalet. It had a large door, with a brass knob and knocker, that didn't seem particularly formidable. He shook his head. "It seems too easy. Go in through the carriage house."

Roland eased out from behind the boulder so he could get a good look at the carriage house. It was built in a similar style to the chalet, with a steep slate roof, rough wood walls, and a stone foundation that rose a yard above the ground to keep the wood siding out of the wet snow. The two buildings were connected by a short breeze-way. The carriage house had large double doors that were unlatched. One was even slightly ajar, but getting in meant crossing forty yards of bare rock, while overhead lurked a monster with claws the size of sickles. He grinned. "Well, I could do that, of course, but surely you don't expect me to . . ."

"Go in through a service entrance," Terry and Alison finished together. Alison added, "If it makes you feel better, I can carry your card in on a silver tray and announce you to the sorcerer."

"Yes, that will be helpful. Come on!"

He grabbed her hand and started the dash for the carriage house. Terry paced them on his charger. Three humans and a horse created enough temptation to stir the gryphon from its perch. It swooped down, four sets of talons ready for combat, and got a jab in the ribs from Terry's lance. But the knight didn't manage a killing strike. The wounded gryphon flew off, and was still circling around for another attack when Roland and Alison reached the door. Roland looked back to see if Terry needed any help. The gryphon was flapping about but staying out of reach of the lance. The knight appeared to be doing fine on his own, so Roland pulled the door shut, leaving it unlatched so Terry could get in. When he turned around, Alison had already entered the chalet.

He edged past a light carriage and buckboard, in through the side door, and quickly found her in the living room. "Don't run off like that. Let's stay together."

Alison pointed. "Look!"

Roland looked. She was pointing to the hearth. Across the stone was spread a number of long, gleaming needles, and curved, wicked-looking hooks. He sucked his breath in sharply. "Torture instruments!"

"No, those are from her sewing bag."

"Oh, right. Then she's been here." He crossed the room and opened the door to the courtyard. It was empty, but he noted that the snow was disturbed. "I think she came in this way." They shut the door and quickly searched the other ground-floor rooms—the dining room, the kitchen, and the pantry. Gloria was not there, nor was there any sign of a sorcerer. At the stairway they both paused. Alison unslung her crossbow. Roland tightened his grip on his ax. She nodded to him and let him go up the stairs first, with Alison two steps behind. The second floor held the sorcerer's study, with a good many maps, racks of potions and powders, a scattering of uncut semiprecious gemstones, and a surprising number of texts on geology and mining. The other rooms seemed to be guest bedrooms. When they discovered that only one of them was locked, they were sure they had found the princess. But they quickly searched the other rooms first, before coming back to it. Two blows with the ax had the door open, and they burst in with their weapons ready.

But this room was empty also. The windows were bare. It didn't even contain furniture.

But it did have another stairway. The door at the top was also locked. "That's got to be it," said Roland.

Alison agreed. "If you're keeping a prisoner, the usual places are the attic or the dungeon, and we haven't seen anything that leads to a lower level."

The door had a simple hasp with a small brass padlock. "I don't need an ax for this," Roland said. He charged up the stairs at full speed and slammed into the door with his shoulder. The hasp tore out of the wood. The door popped open, leaving Roland sprawling on the floor. Alison came and stood over him, covering each corner successively with her crossbow. "Princess Gloria?"

Roland let his eyes get accustomed to the darkness. "She's not here." The attic held nothing more than a few pieces of broken furniture, a couple of trunks of old clothes, holiday decorations and twisted strands of tinsel, and a hideous lamp that had obviously been a gift from someone. The dust that covered everything had not been disturbed, nor had the cobwebs.

"She's got be here someplace," said Alison, once they had returned to the ground level. "Unless she was . . ." She did not want to say "eaten." "Even if she is gone, the Middle-Aged Man of the Mountains should still be here. He couldn't have left. The fire is still burning." They both looked around the empty living room. "This place creeps me out. It looked so nice from the outside, but inside it is spooky. Don't you think it's spooky?"

Roland gave the furniture a cursory glance. "It seems just fine to me. The Kirghiz carpet does a good job of pulling together the colors of the curtains and sofa. I rather like the carved oak wainscoting, although I question the cornices. Probably a later addition. However, that antique Phillipe XIV desk is merely a reproduction." He stopped when he saw Alison giving him a speculative look. "Oh, for God's sake." He grabbed her and kissed her firmly on the lips. "There," he said, letting her go. "Happy now?"

"Mmm-mm," said Alison. Her eyes were shining.

A noise behind them made them jump. It was Terry coming in. He had shed his armor and lance, and was holding the longsword with both hands. He said, "Huh. No horses. Because he has a gryphon, right? But he has a carriage anyway. Did you see it? A fast red two-seater. It looks brand-new."

"I noticed that," said Roland. "And there's a new set of barbells upstairs."

"Yep. He bought a sport carriage and started an exercise program. This guy is middle-aged all right."

"No wonder he went after a young blond. Did you kill the gryphon?"

"No. I tangled with it a couple more times, then it flew off. Where is she?"

"We can't find her," said Alison. "We looked everywhere. She's not here."

Terry sucked in a deep breath, then yelled at the top of his lungs, "GLORIAAAAAAA!"

A faint voice replied, "Down here."

Roland said to Alison, "We were just about to try that, weren't we?"

"Give me the ax." Terry grabbed it away from Roland and passed him the sword.

"But there's no way down," said Alison. "We looked. Is there a secret entrance outside?"

"Behind the bookcase. They always hide one behind the bookcase. There will be an outside exit, too, but here's where we'll look first."

Roland was at the bookcase. "I've seen these in plays. You pull out a book and the secret door swivels open." He scanned the shelves. "What's the book with the least amount of dust on it?" He put his hand on a copy of *Washboard Abs in Thirty Days*. "Here."

He snatched his hand away as the ax struck the shelf, for Terry was demonstrating the highly skilled knights' method of getting through a secret door by chopping a hole in it. Scrolls, codices, folios, and golf trophies went flying everywhere. When he was through, the bookcase lay in splinters and a man-sized opening in the wall revealed a crude stairway, chipped out of stone, leading down into dark rock. Without so much as a pause for breath, Terry rushed into the hole. Roland was right behind him. Alison took a deep breath and waited to see if her heart would stop pounding. It didn't. She followed them anyway.

She arrived at a tunnel carved into the mountain. It was about twice her height and equally wide. Light came from a lamp hanging over the stairway door, and from the far end of the cavern, where it led to open air. Smaller caves branched away into blackness. There was a strong animal smell. One of the caves was closed off with iron bars, secured by a heavy padlock. She saw Terry smash the padlock with the ax, swing the door open, and run inside. Roland was about to follow him when Alison screamed.

She screamed because the Middle-Aged Man of the Mountains had grabbed her arms. She later realized that he had come up right beside her, yet for some reason she hadn't noticed him. His eyes were wild, and there were beads of sweat on his bald spot. He tore the crossbow from her grip, but he wasn't expecting her to fight back, and he dropped it when Alison punched him in the face. He struck her a backhanded blow that sent her sprawling. Then Roland tackled him.

Alison picked up the crossbow. The quarrel had fallen out. She inserted it again, but by then Roland and the sorcerer were rolling around on the ground, hands at each other's throats, too close to each other and moving too fast for her to take aim. The fight didn't last long. It was all over in a matter of seconds. A roaring noise behind Alison broke it up.

Out of the cave charged the ugliest animal Alison had ever seen. It had a body that roughly resembled a lion, but far bigger than any lion had the right to be. All four feet had claws as long as her forearm, and the head had a monstrous beak that looked like it could bite through a hitching post. The wings, even folded, seemed to fill up the tunnel. The whole thing was covered in spines tufted with coarse black down, like the pinfeathers of a vulture with a severe vitamin deficiency, except for a patch of red feathers on the chest. It rushed right at them.

She got off a snap shot with the crossbow and missed, the quarrel passing harmlessly through the feathers. It ignored the attack and simply ran over her. Roland was on his feet by then, trying to pull the longsword out of the scabbard. The beast knocked him down with a blow from its paw. From the stone floor, Alison watched the Middle-Aged Man of the Mountains climb onto the gryphon's back. In a daze she saw them gallop away.

Roland got up first. He put out a hand and lifted Alison to her feet. "Are you all right?"

"Just a little stunned." For a moment she thought he was going to kiss her again, but he looked at the floor and seemed to think better of it. Instead, he bent down and picked up the longsword. Alison picked up the crossbow. Both of them kept their eyes away from the cave. Only silence came from within.

"I guess," said Roland quietly, "I'd better go in and retrieve the bodies. If there's anything left to retrieve." He found he couldn't meet Alison's eyes, so he looked from the cave to the floor and back again.

Alison was doing the same thing. "I'll go upstairs and see if I can find a lantern for you."

Roland nodded. "Maybe bring down some blankets, to cover them. I'd go with you but—I don't know—I feel like I shouldn't leave them."

"I'll take some off the beds." Alison's eyes welled up with tears, and indeed the situation would have turned into a genuine schmaltzfest had not Terry chosen that moment to walk out of the cave unharmed. The Princess Gloria was leaning on his arm.

Roland and Alison stared at her.

"What?" said Gloria. She looked down at herself, then put a hand to her hair. "What?"

"You weren't eaten," said Roland.

"No. I guess it wasn't hungry."

Terry looked around. "Where did it go?"

Roland pointed toward the cavern opening. "It just ran off. The sorcerer was on its back. We couldn't stop him."

"He said it couldn't fly," said Gloria.

"Well, it sure can run fast."

"No matter," said Terry. "The king's troops will track him down soon enough." He put his arm around Gloria's shoulders. "The important thing is that Gloria—um—the Princess Gloria, is safe."

Alison was looking at Gloria speculatively. "Yes. So why didn't the gryphon eat you?"

"I told you," Gloria said defensively. "It wasn't hungry."

"Oh yes. That's right."

"Well it wasn't!"

Alison looked at Roland, and so did Terry. The knight gave Roland a threatening stare. "Now see here," he said. "I am a knight and a soldier in the Royal Guard. It is my sworn duty to defend the princess, both her life *and her honor*. Is that clear?"

"Why are you looking at me?" said Roland. "I didn't say a word."

"Yes, but it's the way you're not saying it that I don't like."

"I'm sorry," broke in Alison, soothingly. "It's my fault. I didn't mean to cast aspersions. Might I suggest we all get out of this dungeon, or whatever this is, and go upstairs for a cup of tea?"

Roland looked as if he was about to say something, but he held himself in check until they reached the living room. As soon as he came through the hole in the wall, he said, "Princess Gloria, permit me to introduce myself. I am Roland Westfield, your fiancé."

Gloria was facing the fireplace, still clutching Terry's arm. She blinked twice before turning around and extending her hand to Roland. "Mr. Westfield. How kind of you to come."

Roland took her hand and bowed over it. "I'm sorry we could not arrive sooner."

"We have much to discuss." Gloria gave him the kind of smile that women use in public places, where the lips are curled up but the eyes send the message that trouble is coming. Roland saw it and didn't know what it meant. Alison didn't know either, but she jumped in.

"I'm so glad to see that you are unharmed, Princess Gloria."

"Thank you, Alison. And how is your father?"

"Baron Wayless is fine, thank you."

"What?" said Terry and Roland together, and if they had been performing as a comedy duo, their double takes could not have been synchronized more perfectly.

"Umm," said Alison. "I mean he's still sick, of course, and he took a blow to the head, but other than that he . . ."

"Who are you?" said Roland.

Gloria looked mystified. "I'm sorry. Were you waiting to be introduced? Alison, this is Roland Westfield. Mr. Westfield, this is the honorable Alison Wayless, daughter of Baron Wayless."

"Baron Wayless is your father?"

"Why, yes," said Alison. "Didn't I tell you that? I'm sure I must have mentioned it."

"You said you were a cook," said Terry.

"I am a cook."

"I thought you were . . ."

"Wasn't your father involved in the kidnapping?" interrupted Roland.

"Oh no," said Gloria. "It was Count Bussard all along. Look! My needlepoint." She ran to the fireplace, where implements and bits of lace were still spread out, and picked up her bag. "I'm so glad I didn't lose this."

"It's very pretty," said Roland.

"Sir Terry," said Gloria, turning to the knight. "Might I have a word with you in private?" Her voice made Alison think of candy, in the sense that the words managed to be sweet while also hard and brittle.

"Uh, sure," said Terry.

"I'll go into the kitchen and look for tea things," said Alison hastily.

"I'll help you," said Roland, who could sense an argument coming as well as the next man. They both gave Terry a sympathetic look and eased out as quickly as they could do so without appearing to flee.

Gloria waited until they left, closed the door behind them, and made sure it shut firmly. Then she turned on Terry. "Terry, what is he doing here! *What is he doing here!*"

Terry had seen this coming, but his mouth didn't get out the words he wanted to say. "It was unavoidable. I couldn't leave him behind."

"Couldn't leave him behind!" Gloria's voice rose. "Terry, did you forget that the whole point of this exercise was to cut him out of the picture? What on earth possessed you to bring him along?"

"Keep your voice down," Terry hissed. "I didn't bring him along. He decided to set out on his own. It was just plain, damn, dumb luck that he chose the right direction. I had to join him to keep track of him so I could make sure I got to you first. Everything would have been fine if you hadn't been kidnapped for real."

"All right." Gloria took a deep breath. "All right, I'm

sorry I yelled at you." She sat on the couch and patted the seat next to her. Terry sat down. Gloria rewarded him with a long and heartfelt kiss, then said, "We need a plan. Fill me in on what happened."

Terry gave her a compressed description of his partnership with Roland, the assault on the Baron's manor, the discovery of Alison, the infiltration of the Count's castle, and the assault on the sorcerer's mountain hideout. He resisted the temptation to exaggerate his feats, but ordinary human nature did cause him to downplay the roles of Roland and Alison. Gloria was suitably impressed. She was disappointed that he didn't find the trail of lace she dropped for him, but gratified that Terry had made use of the rope she wove. She was especially interested in Terry's explanation for her kidnapping.

"The way I see it," he told her, "is that Bussard didn't intend to grab you at all. He actually wanted to kidnap Alison."

"He said as much to me. But why?"

"He wanted their land. My guess is that Alison is the sole heir. Bussard was the magistrate for Bornewald. With the Baron dead, he could appoint himself, or one of his cronies, to be her guardian and control the land until she came of age. By that time he'd have figured out a way to transfer the land to himself."

"Could he really get away with that?"

"Oh sure. You know how it is when you're a knight. One of my duties is to ride around the country upholding justice and defending the downtrodden. And let me tell you, it doesn't take long before you've seen every dirty trick in the book." Terry leaned back and stretched out his legs. "Bussard was waiting for Wayless to die, but he must have been afraid that Alison would get married and then she'd be out of his reach. He probably decided he couldn't wait any longer. He wanted to take her into custody before the Baron kicked the bucket."

Gloria turned on her back and rested her head in Terry's lap. "I'm not sorry that Bussard is dead."

"Neither am I. I'd like to know where the Middle-Aged Man of the Mountains went."

"Not to worry. He'll be caught, or he'll flee the country. He's probably fleeing the country right now. Mmmmm." She closed her eyes as Terry stroked her hair, then opened them again. "Our immediate concern is what you and I are going to do."

"It's just that I have this feeling." Terry looked around the room, the scattered books, the reclining armchair, the fireplace. There was something tugging at his brain, but it wouldn't show itself. Something he was forgetting.

"What?"

"I don't know. Something is wrong, but I can't think of it."

"Then think of something else, and it will come up. That always works for me. Think about us."

"What did you have in mind?"

"We'll have to elope," said Gloria, sadly. "I was hoping to avoid it, but we always knew it might be our last resort."

"Yes. I'm sorry. I know you wanted the big wedding."

"Oh, that's not so important. But we'll be cut out of society. We'll have to bury ourselves in the country and stay out of sight for a few years. No more invitations for us. Mother will be so mad, and of course, no hostess will dare cross her. Nor the Westfields, either. They'll be very upset."

"I don't know about the Westfields. They might be

more accepting. Roland seems pretty happy with Alison. Maybe he doesn't know it, but he's in love with her."

"Really?"

"I'm sure of it. Before we came up here, they were arguing in a restaurant."

Gloria sat up suddenly. She arranged herself by Terry's side and looked at him thoughtfully. "Did they talk to each other? Without arguing, I mean?"

"Um, yes, at the inn and places."

"Other people saw them?"

"Yes. Why?"

"Were they ever alone together?"

"If they were together, they weren't alone."

"You know what I mean."

"I suppose. I wasn't with them all the time."

Gloria's brow wrinkled. "I wonder if we could get some sort of breach-of-promise thing going. Even if it is only a rumor, it could be enough to cause a scandal. Mother would break off the engagement . . ."

"Cancel that idea!" Terry's voice was stern. "Roland Westfield is an honorable guy. He thought you were in danger, and he came here to try to rescue you. We are *not* going to smear his reputation."

Gloria looked contrite. She threw her arms around Terry. "You're right. You're right, sweetie. I was just thinking about us."

"I understand. In fact, I'm going to talk to Roland right now." Terry set Gloria aside and stood up. "Gloria, I'm going to tell him right out. I've had enough of these plots and subterfuges. I'll tell him that we decided to get married, and that's all there is to it. It's what I should have done right from the start."

"Oh, Terry! I'll find a way to make it up to you. I know this will dishonor you as a knight. I only wish girls had a choice in these matters. Then we could break our own engagements."

"That would certainly make courtship easier."

"I hope Roland will be civilized. It's quite a loss for him."

"What do you mean?"

"Really, Terry. I know Alison is very sweet, and rather pretty, in a simple country-girl sort of way, but—look at her. You have to admit she's a bit on the skinny side."

"Um, right. Right." There were not many acceptable responses that a man could make to a statement like that, but Terry thought quickly and came up with one of them. "But remember, Roland hadn't seen you before he met Alison. And even now, he hasn't seen you at your best."

"Oh my God!" Gloria jumped up and frantically cast her eyes about, looking for a mirror. "I'm a mess. Where's a hairbrush? Oh Terry, look at me."

With her tousled hair, smeared lipstick, and torn clothing, Terry actually thought she looked pretty hot, in a down-and-dirty bad girl sort of way. He also knew that this wasn't the time to say so. "You look fine. Really. I'll go talk to Roland."

He left her searching for a washroom and made his way to the kitchen. Roland and Alison were both bending over the stove, their heads close together, trying to light some kindling and talking in low voices. They both straightened up when he came in, looking a little guilty. Alison said, "I guess she was pretty angry."

"We could hear her from in here," said Roland. "We couldn't make out the words, but she sounded upset."

"But she'll get over it," Alison said encouragingly. "She's had a rough time, but it wasn't your fault. She probably doesn't realize the risks that you took for her. A cup of tea and a nap, and she'll feel a lot better. Roland and I will make sure the king knows the whole story. We'll tell him that you rescued her as soon as you could."

"Um, thank you," said Terry, who didn't follow this.

"The Princess Gloria is a tremendously fine girl," said Roland. "I don't know much about her myself, but everyone kept telling me what a great person she is. My family just raved about her."

"She came to visit my father, and she was very nice. Very warm and personable."

"I don't disagree," said Terry. "Is there a point to this?"

Roland looked at Alison. She nervously shifted the teakettle on the stove and fiddled with the damper. Eventually she met his eyes with a "go ahead" look. He transferred his gaze to Terry. "See, I've been doing a lot of thinking lately, and even though the Princess Gloria has many fine qualities, I'm not sure that she's really the right girl for me. Don't get me wrong. I'm sure she would be a wonderful partner for the right man. It's just that I don't feel that I'm ready to get married yet." He looked back at Alison, who nodded to him encouragingly. "This past few days, what with the travel and adventures and all, I've learned a lot about myself, and I think I need to take some time to sort it out."

"I see," said Terry. "Roland, it sounds to me more like you have your heart set on someone else."

"No!" said Roland and Alison together, and Roland added, "That isn't the case at all."

"I thought perhaps you and Alison . . ."

"No, it's not like that. Alison has nothing to do with this decision."

"No," said Alison.

"I don't want to leave anyone with the impression that Alison goes around breaking up other people's engagements. Of course she doesn't. This is purely my own idea."

"It is."

"I have no interest in marrying Alison instead of Gloria."

"He doesn't."

"Not right away, at least."

"We have to get to know each other first," said Alison.

"Although," Roland continued, "her noble birth would certainly help smooth things over with my family, if it came to that."

"I understand," said Terry. "And I suspect there is a solution to your problem. In fact, I was thinking . . ."

"You could marry Gloria," interrupted Roland.

"I beg your pardon?"

"Marry the princess." Roland held up his hands. "No wait, Terry. Don't say anything until you hear me out. You probably haven't considered this, but the man who rescues a princess from mortal danger earns the right to her hand in marriage. If you take sole credit for the rescue, you can demand that she marry you."

"Marry the Princess Gloria?" said Terry. "Me?" He gave Roland and Alison a skeptical look. "That sounds pretty far-fetched."

"Roland is right," said Alison. "This tradition about rescuing and marrying a princess, it isn't just a tradition in Medulla. It's more like common law. I probably shouldn't tell you this, but Gloria didn't really want to marry Roland. She had another boy in mind that she was hoping would rescue her first, just so she could marry him instead."

"Really?" said Terry. "Who?"

"I don't know. She didn't tell me his name. It doesn't matter, because he's out of the picture now. If you're the rescuer, she has to marry you."

"*If* I'm the rescuer?"

The slightly sarcastic intonation was lost on Roland. "Sure, Terry. Think about it. When you were fighting the thugs at the Baron's manor, I was upstairs with Alison. If the princess saw anyone, she only saw you. She doesn't know you were just there to assist me. At the Count's castle, she might have seen you from that balcony, but she had no way of knowing that I was already inside by that time."

"Right," said Alison. "And the same thing happened here. All she knows is that you charged into the monster's cage to rescue her. If Roland and I say that we didn't arrive until after it was all over, who's to say any different?"

"Well, it's certainly an intriguing idea," said Terry. "But do you really think she'll go for it?"

"Oh sure. She doesn't really have a choice. Just act confident and tell her how it is going to be."

"Some new clothes will help," said Roland. "You might as well put your best foot forward. I can give you some advice there."

"And I'll help you with your hair," offered Alison. "A good haircut makes all the difference. But don't worry. A lot of girls aren't into looks."

"Thank you!" snapped Terry.

"He looks fine," said Roland. "Plenty of girls like big, tough-looking guys. Wait. Oh, damn it all. I just remembered something." Roland pulled up a wooden chair and sat at the kitchen table. "Forget it, Alison. He won't do it."

"Yes, he will." Alison looked beseechingly at Terry. "Won't you?"

"I suppose that, under the circumstances . . ."

"He's a knight," explained Roland. "We can't expect him to take part in a plan like this, to marry a girl under false pretenses. Not just as a favor to us. It would be dishonorable."

"Uh," said Terry. "Yes, in a sense that is true, but where young love is concerned . . ."

"This is the king's daughter, after all. Terry swore an oath of fealty to the king. He's not going to lie to his sovereign."

"Not normally, no. But I could make an exception . . ."

"He doesn't have to lie," Alison told Roland. "We will. All he has to do is keep quiet and go along with it." She turned to Terry. "Remember, Roland is of the merchant class. They can do anything they want—lie, cheat, steal, bribe, swindle—if someone objects all they have to do is say, 'It's just good business.' "

Roland cleared his throat. "That's . . . that's not one hundred percent true."

"All right then," Terry said loudly. He strode forward and put a hand on each of their shoulders. "Roland, Alison," he said, looking from one to the other. "We've been through a lot in the last twenty-four hours, and I think we've made an excellent team. I'm grateful for all you've done. We might not all be here if we hadn't worked together. If it's important to you that I marry the Princess Gloria, you can count on me."

Alison threw her arms around him and hugged him gratefully. Roland somberly shook his hand. When he had accepted their thanks, Terry said, "I guess I'd better go in and tell her."

"No," said Roland. "Thank you, Terry, but I'll do the job myself. It's a poor thing for a gentleman to break his engagement, but if I'm going to do it, I'll not do it by proxy." He squared up his shoulders and marched to the drawing room, shutting the kitchen door firmly behind him.

Alison immediately ran to the door and bent down to the keyhole, but Terry got in front of her and looked at her sternly. She had to pretend she had bent over to pick a piece of straw off the floor. Nonetheless, they both strained their ears, trying to discern words from the barely audible murmurings that came through the wood. Eventually they heard the sound of Roland's boots returning. Terry opened the door for him, and Alison looked at him questioningly. Roland shrugged. "It's done," was all he said. He took Alison's hand.

"What did she say?"

"Nothing. She cried."

"She cried?" asked Terry.

Roland nodded. "I suppose I should have expected it. She didn't cry exactly, but there were tears streaming down her face, and she was making those choking noises, like girls do when they're holding back sobs."

"She'll get over it," said Alison. "In the long run it's all for the best."

"Right," said Terry. "Well, the princess and I have a lot to talk about now, and I shouldn't put it off any longer. I guess I'd better find out how she feels about me." He went into the drawing room, where Gloria immediately buried her face in his chest.

"Oh Terry," she said, trying to smother her laughter in his jacket. "You should have seen his face! He looked so grave. I thought for certain I was going to give it all away. I had to bite my lip to keep from laughing. My goodness, Terry, what on earth did you say to him?"

"Nothing much. I just explained the situation to him, and he realized he had no choice in the matter. I thought he took it pretty well."

"You're a born diplomat, darling." Gloria turned her face up for a long and soulful kiss. Then, with her tongue still in his mouth, walked him backward until he toppled onto the couch. She climbed on top of him, straddled his waist, and slipped her hands inside his shirt. She bent down to nuzzle his neck. "Terry," she whispered.

"Hmmm?"

"Do you remember last year, after the Midsummer Fair, when we slipped away from everyone and climbed up the south tower?"

"Yes?"

"We were in that little room, with the soft spring breeze blowing through the windows, and the smell of apple blossoms, and the whole of the city spread out beneath us?"

"Mm-mmm." His eyes were closed, as he enjoyed the feeling of her lips against his ear.

"Remember how romantic it was?"

"Mm-mmm." Her breasts were squashed against him.

"The scented air," murmured Gloria. "The setting sun, the music coming up from below?"

"Mm-mmm."

"Just the two of us?"

"Mm-mmm."

"Okay, it doesn't count if it's only her mouth, right?"

"Right," said Terry, eyes suddenly wide open.

"That's what you told me."

"That's the way I've always heard it. Yes!"

Gloria put both hands in Terry's hair and turned his head until the two of them were eyeball-to-eyeball. "So the gryphon just wasn't hungry, right?"

"Right! That's got to be it. It's the only explanation."

The princess relaxed. "Just checking." She snuggled closed to him and nibbled his earlobe again, transferred her lips from his ear to his mouth. She gave him a long, deep kiss, really getting into it, until she pulled her face away, frowned, sat back up, and said, "What's wrong?"

"Nothing."

"Terry, your attention was wandering. I could tell. When a girl who looks like me gives a boy the kind of kiss I just gave you, and his mind is somewhere else, something is seriously wrong."

"Okay." Terry sat up. "Something is wrong. Something important. Something I'm missing." He looked around the room. "But I don't know what it is."

"Something in this room?" Gloria tried to follow his gaze.

"No. Yes. I don't know." He let his eyes linger on the fireplace again. Suddenly he pointed to it. "Girls! Virgins! Lace!"

Gloria looked at the hearth, which still held her needles

and a few scraps of lace. She put a hand to her mouth. "Oh no," she whispered. "The Autumn Ball!"

It was a ride that would become legendary in Medulla. They rode all day and all night, on the fastest horses money could buy, four good riders in hot pursuit of an evil sorcerer and a magic monster. They didn't rest. They ran the horses until they were exhausted and blowing foam, then they bought more at the next town and rode on. They took unthinkable risks, galloping full tilt over uneven ground, at night, in deep woods and shadows, jumping over streams, hedges, and gates. They didn't split up, and they didn't slow down, trusting that if one horse stumbled and fell, or two, or three, at least one of them would make it through to the city and warn the Guard. It was during the periods when Roland was paying for the horses, and the others were changing over the saddles and bridles, that Terry and Gloria had a chance to explain to Alison.

"The Autumn Ball is lace intensive," said Terry. "Even the men wear some lace, a bit on our cuffs and collars. Of course, girls wear lace at other times, but it's a tradition of the Autumn Ball to wear a lot of lace. Some girls wear dresses that are nothing but lace. It's pretty cool," he added, his thoughts turning inward. "You almost think you can see right through it but they never actually show their . . ."

Gloria interrupted him. "Girls come from all over Medulla to sell their lace. The dressmakers and seamstresses will be working right up to the last minute, and the girls will be tatting lace right up to the evening of the ball. Medulla is famous for its lace fashions."

"But I still don't see the connection," puzzled Alison. Her new horse was not cooperating. She waited for it to exhale before tightening the cinch. "There are women everywhere. Why now? Why lace?"

"Because the finest lace is made by young girls. You need girls who are old enough to have the patience for needlework but have sharp eyes and nimble fingers to make the tiny knots. They work on it in the evenings, after the chores are done. We'll see hundreds of them coming in from the farms with their year's work. Just the kind of girls he's looking for."

"It's their spending money for the year," added Terry.

"For one month of the year the city is overflowing with young virgins," said Roland. He had finished paying for the horses and returned in time to catch the end of the explanation. His pouch of coins had been steadily diminishing. "Every street will be a giant feeding trough for that gryphon if we don't catch it."

"We'll catch it," promised Terry. He swung onto a horse and started off. The others followed.

But they didn't catch it. The beast seemed tireless. They rode as hard as the horses could stand it, but they didn't even catch sight of the gryphon. It, and the sorcerer, stayed well ahead of them.

"Maybe he lied to me," said Gloria, when they stopped briefly to water the horses. She had to lean on her horse to support herself. Her bottom was sore, and her joints were aching. "The sorcerer told me that this gryphon couldn't fly yet, but maybe it already flew away." She bent over the trough and splashed water on her face.

The boys were as tired as the girls. Terry was in the saddle, holding himself erect with visible effort. He pointed to long scores in the hard dirt. "It didn't fly," he said. "It's leaving tracks that even I can follow. There's no mistaking those claws. And the trail is getting fresher. We're gaining on it."

"Why hasn't anyone else seen him?"

"Sorcerers have ways of not being noticed if they don't want to be. But I think other people have sounded the alarm. It's just that we're riding faster than the news can travel."

"Where is he going?" asked Alison. "To the Autumn Ball? It's not for days."

"Probably one of the other parties, I expect," said Roland.

"The Autumn Ball *is* the big party," explained Gloria. "The nobility will gather in the palace ballroom. But most of the girls will party in town. There are all sorts of other events going on the whole week leading up to the ball." She added, with just a trace of pride, "Even people from Occipital come to Sulcus for the parties."

"The streets will be full of girls," Terry continued for her. "They go wild in town. All the money they get for their lace doesn't go home with them. Ha! You can bet a lot fewer virgins leave Sulcus each year than come in." He saw Gloria giving him a stern look. "Um, so I've heard," he added hastily. "Let's ride."

They were still some threescore miles from the city when they finally sighted the Middle-Aged Man of the Mountains. They caught but a glimpse of him the first time, disappearing around a bend, but it was enough to make them spur their horses to greater speed. To no avail—the gryphon kept its lead. Throughout the day they sighted it again and again, vanishing over a hill or around a corner. It was almost an even match. The horses were faster, but the gryphon never seemed to stop. Slowly, slowly, they narrowed the gap, but the giant beast with the scraggly feathers and the balding man on its back stayed obstinately ahead. By the time they reached the outskirts of the city, it was only a few hundred feet ahead of them.

But that was lead enough. Dusk was falling as the Middle-Aged Man of the Mountains raced through the city gates. In part that was a good thing, for most of the young girls were gone. In a short time they would be spilling into the streets, chatting and laughing in groups, on their way to the dinners that preceded each night of dancing and music, but just then they were indoors preparing for the evening's parties. A few older lacemakers remained on the sidewalks, trying to make a few more pennies, working under streetlamps to save the price of candles. The downside of dusk was that it became hard to see, especially in the shadows of the buildings. Several times Terry, who knew the city as well as anyone, lost the Middle-Aged Man of the Mountains as he dodged among the narrow streets. The sorcerer seemed to know where he was going. But by luck and inspired guesswork Terry found him again as the gryphon charged up the front stairs of a long, classically styled stone building. It was a double block of apartments that ran alongside the royal palace. The Middle-Aged Man of the Mountains leaped off the animal's back and ran into the eastern wing of the building. The gryphon, now riderless, bounded into the west wing.

Terry arrived only moments behind them. He bounced to the ground and grabbed the ax from behind the saddle. "Get the sorcerer," he shouted, as the others rode up. "I'll get the gryphon." He disappeared into the apartment block. Roland and Alison left their horses untethered and ran into the other wing. Gloria, unsure where to go, looked from one door to the other, then followed Terry.

Behind them the air filled with the smell of cooking and woodsmoke. Storefronts shuttered their windows, and their shopgirls ran excitedly into the streets. In a nearby courtyard, a quintet of musicians started a lively tune. The evening's round of parties had begun.

"No," said Jennifer firmly, pushing George's hands away. She began to button her blouse back up. Then she saw George's disappointed look and changed her voice to a more gentle tone. "It's been a wonderful day, Georgy. Let's not spoil it."

"It doesn't spoil it," said George. "It makes it better." It was the oldest and lamest reply a man could make to a statement like that. No man in the entire history of courtship has ever had a lick of success with it, and George didn't expect that he would either. But he felt that he had to say it anyway. When you lived in a conservative country like Medulla, and especially if you were dating a princess, you knew you weren't going to get anywhere with her without at least an engagement ring. But still you had to make a pass at the girl, even though she would pretend to be offended. If you didn't try out some moves, she might start to wonder if there was something wrong with you, or if you thought there was something wrong with her.

They were in an apartment that George had started renting a few months ago. It was a small studio, a single

room close to the palace, insignificant compared to
George's real home in the city, the lavish mansion near
Marlington Park where he stayed when he was not at his
estate. He got it so he and Jennifer could meet in comfort,
and more importantly, in private. Even his valet didn't
know about the studio. George told the landlord he was
an artist and needed a private, quiet place to sketch. To
augment the deception that he was in an artistic profes-
sion, he left unpaid bills scattered about and kept the
place well stocked with booze. He had a bulging liquor
cabinet, an assortment of mismatched glassware, and a
rack filled with bottles of cheap wine, along with a couple
of good ones that they actually planned to drink. Aside
from that there was little in the way of furniture, merely a
vanity, a few end tables with lamps scattered about, and
the most luxurious love seat he could get his hands on
without stimulating undue gossip.

A love seat is designed to hold two people. The man's
side is the side with the back. The woman's side has no
back, in the hope that the woman will eventually tire of
sitting up straight and be forced to lean against the man for
support. George relaxed against the backrest while Jennifer went to the mirror and restored her hair and makeup.

"It's not that I'm uptight or a prude, Georgie," she
said, over her shoulder. She ran a hairbrush through her
light brown hair, which somehow had managed to become disheveled in the course of the afternoon. "You
know that. And I'm not a slave to old-fashioned notions
of morality. I can decide these things for myself."

"Right," said George.

"I *want* to do it with you, Georgie, I really do. I'm
burning with desire for you." She turned to look at him.

"Georgie," she said earnestly, "You know how much I love you."

"I love you, too, baby."

"But I don't want it to be casual, darling. When the time is right for us, we'll know it. I want the first time to be special, don't you? I want . . ." She paused to take a deep breath.

You want it to mean something, thought George.

"I want it to mean something," said Jennifer.

Right, George almost said, but caught himself just in time. It was important not to agree when girls said things like this. Because once you agreed that the two of you weren't going to do it, you were stuck. Later on you might get lucky—she might get drunk or something and give you a chance with her—and you couldn't go back on your word. So you had to say something agreeable without actually agreeing.

"I understand how you feel," he said.

Satisfied with the answer, Jennifer blew him a kiss. She turned back to the mirror. "Now I have to go," she said, slurring a little because she was applying lip gloss from a little pot. George watched appreciatively. He understood full well that women didn't wear makeup to look better for men. They wore it to look better to other women. Even so, glossy red lipstick was always a turn-on. "No, don't come with me, Georgie. We've spent too much time together today, and people might talk. We need to leave separately. I'll see you at the party tonight?"

"I'll be waiting for you," George promised. He finished lacing up his breeches, gave his boots a quick dust-off, and looked around for his sword. It was hanging on a rack beneath his hat. He checked his look in a mirror. He was wearing a loose shirt with ruffles on the front and blouson sleeves. He didn't care for it much, but he'd heard that girls thought pirate shirts were sexy.

Jennifer gave her hair a final pat, slid back the bolt on the heavy door, and opened it a crack. She didn't want to be seen leaving a man's room, so she peered out the door first to see in anyone was around. She saw a gryphon trotting down the hall.

She wasn't afraid, because it was just too hard to believe. She shut the door, shook her head twice, as though to clear it, and opened the door again. This time she stuck her entire head out. This time she became afraid.

It was huge. It was as big as a dragon. It had the body of a lion, but bigger than any lion she'd ever heard of. It filled the corridor. Its powerful shoulders brushed against both walls. All four feet had great, curved claws, and the great beak was clearly designed for ripping chunks of flesh. The wings were folded close to the body, and the feathers looked sickly for some reason, but it was undoubtedly a gryphon. It stopped. It looked directly at her. The great beak opened, revealing a slimy black tongue. A column of fear rose up inside her, and through the column bubbled a memory, something from her school days, something about the diet of the gryphon.

In one continuous blur of movement she slammed the door, shot the bolt, turned, and leaped on George. Astonished, he stumbled backward and sprawled on the loveseat, where she hiked up her dress and straddled him with lithe thighs. Her small fists grabbed his collar and ripped his shirt open. "Georgie," she yelled, "let's do it!"

"What?" said George. Her hands were fumbling at his trousers. "You just said you wanted to wait."

"I changed my mind. A girl can change her mind, can't she?" A sniffing noise came from outside the door. It was followed by scratching. "I need you right now. How do you get these off?"

"You have to unlace . . . what's that noise?"

"Ignore it," yelled Jennifer, grinding her pelvis against him. "Here, play with these!" She put both hands on the front of her bodice and ripped.

"Jennifer, there's something out there . . . wow!" said George as her breasts sprang free among a shower of small pearl buttons. She shoved his face between them as her fingers fumbled frantically with the cord on his breeches. From behind the door the gryphon gave an ugly growl.

"I can't get them off! Georgie, I can't get them off."

"You've got the laces into a knot," said George. His voice was muffled by her breasts. "Just take it easy. I'll get them."

"I can't wait," yelled Jennifer. "I've got to have you inside me right away!"

I need to get more of these shirts, thought George. "Hey, that's really flattering, Jenny, but it will be better if you relax and take it slow. What is that?"

The scratching turned into a scraping. The heavy door was shaking on its hinges. Jennifer spotted George's dagger lying on the end table. She scrambled over him and grabbed it. George flailed away at petticoats and velvet skirt until he could surface for air. His head came up just in time to see a dagger descend toward his crotch. "Yaaah!"

His ardor evaporated as he scrambled backward in horror. The dagger missed its intended destination and plunged between his legs, into the love seat upholstery. "Gah!"

"Oops. Sorry. Hold still, will you?"

"Jennifer, what are you doing? Are you crazy? Put that down!"

"I've got it now, don't worry." Jennifer sliced through his waistband and tossed the dagger aside. "Just get it out." She fished around in his underwear and grabbed.

"Ow! Not so tight! Let go!"

Crack, went the door, followed by the sound of splintering wood. The center panel split open. A foot the size of a hand basket, with four long claws, came through. Jennifer screamed and dove over the love seat, curling herself into a ball behind it. The claw withdrew, ripping a splintered hole on the way out. George stared at it with complete bafflement, his mental transmission still trying to shift gears. The gryphon shoved its head through the door and snarled.

Lord George, literally caught with his pants down, demonstrated remarkably good instincts for such circumstances. Without quite knowing what he was doing, he grabbed a lamp from the end table and flung it at the gryphon's beak. His aim was little high, but no matter. The glass lamp hit the doorframe above the beast's head and exploded with a soft *whooomp*, showering the gryphon with burning oil. Most animals react negatively to fire. The gryphon was, thankfully, no exception. It gave a screech of pain and anger, long, drawn-out, and chilling, and twisted its head, trying to shake off the oil. Unable to do so, it pulled its head out of the door. Jennifer and George could hear it screeching and screaming, banging against the walls and ceiling, and then the clicking of claws on the floor and the rustling of feathers as it moved away. The noise faded off into silence.

Burning oil had ignited the wool carpet. Varnish was already blistering on the doorframe, and the room was filling with smoke. George grabbed his coat off the rack. He hastily beat out the flames with one hand, while holding his pants up with the other. Jennifer knew enough to wait until fire was out before she opened a window, then she fanned in some fresh air. This helped to clear away most of the smoke, along with the acrid smell of burned fur and burned feathers. With the flames gone, George threw the remains of his coat on the floor and gave Jenny a questioning look. She was about to explain when they heard more movement in the hall.

Quickly His Lordship fumbled his sword belt off the coatrack. His trousers fell down around his ankles. He kicked them off in frustration, pulled his blade from the scabbard, and stood ready. Jennifer ran to the love seat again and crouched behind it. Gloria poked her head in through the shattered door.

"Oh hi, Lord George. Hi, Jenny. I'm back. Nice place you have here. You didn't happen to see a gryphon go by, did you? A big one, kind of scraggly, with a bad attitude?"

Jennifer rose from behind the love seat. Dazedly she pointed down the hall. George used his sword to indicate the same direction.

"Thanks, Jenny." Gloria put an arm through the hole and plucked the sword from George's hand. "You don't mind if I borrow this, do you, Lord George?" He shook his head. "Thank you so much. I have to run. See you later." Then she, too, disappeared into the smoke.

George, totally confused, sat down heavily in the love seat. He looked at Jennifer. She was leaning over the love seat, trying to cover her bare breasts with her hands, while the light from the remaining lamp threw a soft glow on her skin. Proof that hope lives eternal, George held his arms out to her. "Okay, darling, I'm ready now."

"No!" said Jennifer.

Alison looked terrible. Her long brown hair was windblown into a mass of knots and tangles, her dress was spattered with mud thrown up by galloping hooves, her shoes were little more than cakes of dirt, and beads of perspiration carved channels in the road grime on her face. Her eyes were twin mirrors of exhaustion and stress. She looked like a madwoman who had escaped from a lunatic asylum by hiding tunneling under a compost heap. Nonetheless, she had no trouble getting past the doorman in the second apartment block. In fact, he took great pains to get out of her way. So did everyone else she encountered. "People respect a girl with a crossbow," she told Roland. "I'm going to have to get myself one of these."

"The first step is to raise an alarm," said Roland. "Alert any guards you can find. Then search this floor and work up. I'll go to the top floor and work down." He left her and ran up four flights of stone stairs. It opened onto a long, narrow corridor. It was lined with apartment doors. He found the Middle-Aged Man of the Mountains right away.

I should have known he'd go up here, he told himself. *Why do sorcerers always like the high places?*

All the doors on the fourth level were closed and dark, indicating that their owners had not yet returned home to light the lamps. Except for one door, which had a thin gleam coming from near the floor, and a faint glow at the keyhole. Roland silently edged up to it. Cautiously, he knelt to the keyhole. Looking through, he saw a furnished sitting room. It had an armchair, a sofa, an end table, and a small round table with two chairs. A middle-aged man was sitting at the table. In back of him were two large casement windows.

Roland straightened up and put one hand on the hilt of his sword. With the other hand he tried the doorknob. It was unlocked. Ever so gently he twisted the knob. It made no sound. He eased the door open an inch and put his eye to the crack.

The middle-aged man was working by the light of a table lamp. He had two shot glasses in front of him, a dropper, a folded towel, and a bottle of amber liquid that Roland guessed was whiskey—Roland couldn't make out the brand. The Middle-Aged Man of the Mountains poured whiskey into each of the shot glasses until they were half-full. Then, as Roland watched, he removed a tiny vial from his pocket. With the dropper, he added a single drop of red liquid to one of the shot glasses. Then he very carefully corked the bottle and put it back in his pocket.

Roland started to draw his sword, but stopped when he realized that he couldn't pull it from the scabbard without making a noise. He looked at the door. It opened inward. He stepped back, took a deep breath, kicked the door open with one booted foot, and drew his sword at the same time. The door swung open and hit the wall with a crash that startled Roland, but didn't seem to alarm the sorcerer in the least. Stepping inside, Roland pointed his sword at the Middle-Aged Man of the Mountains and shouted, "Don't move."

He had no idea if this was the correct procedure, but that was how they did it in the theatre. The Middle-Aged Man of the Mountains took it calmly enough. He leaned back in his chair, and said, "You're out of shape. You're still panting from climbing the stairs. I ran up four flights, and I wasn't even breathing hard."

"Yeah, great. I suppose next you're going to brag about how much you bench-press. Save it for the courts." Roland waggled the point of his sword in what he hoped was a threatening manner. "I'm bringing you in."

"My, what a pretty sword." The sorcerer casually pushed his chair back from the table. "All those nice jewels, and silver filigree. A custom job?"

"Yes, and so what?" snapped Roland defensively. "I appreciate good craftsmanship, okay?"

"So do I, my young friend. That's why I carry this one." The Middle-Aged Man of the Mountains drew his sword in one motion, so quickly it hissed in the air. He did this without even rising from his chair, which is not an easy thing to do. It caught Roland by surprise. He involuntarily took a step back. The sorcerer smiled.

"I took this from a royal courtier in Angostura. Apparently one of my little projects displeased him, and he felt constrained to make noises about bringing me to face the king's justice and so forth. He was an arrogant sort of fellow, but he had quite a reputation as a duelist. Skilled in all the arts of defense, they said. Younger than myself, but very experienced for his age, they said. I rather liked the idea of taking his sword as a trophy. He was the fourth man I killed."

"Uh-huh," said Roland. He didn't know how to respond to this. It didn't sound good, though.

"But there's no need to rush into a fight. We still have a little time." The Middle-Aged Man of the Mountains stood up and sheathed his sword as quickly and smoothly as he drew it. "Come to the window."

Roland moved cautiously forward, staying out of sword's reach. He edged around the sofa until he was able to look out one of the windows, down at a gated courtyard, protected by a wrought-iron fence. To one side was the palace, with its brightly lit windows and balconies, and ahead of him was a small square with a lamppost in the center, surrounded by four cast-iron benches. It was the square that marked the beginning of Couture Street. A gaggle of teenage girls had gathered under the streetlamp. They were chattering gaily, oblivious to the chill, damp, autumn weather. Somewhere a band was playing. Strains of music wafted from the street up to the window. "Good band," Roland said absently.

"They're too damn loud," said the Middle-Aged Man of the Mountains. "And all their music sounds the same."

The window was misty with condensation. Roland rubbed it with his sleeve and peered out. More girls were approaching the square.

"Come to sell the day's needlework," said the Middle-Aged Man of the Mountains. "I kick myself for not thinking of this sooner. My pets like the mountains, so I located myself out there. That's where I'll find the gold, after all. Except that out in the country it was taking years to harvest the odd stray girl. I don't know why the peasants think their children are so valuable, they breed replace-ments quickly enough. But no matter. Here my beast will find enough in one night."

"So what? Good Lord, mister, there's a whole city full of guards and policemen and knights and soldiers out there. By morning, your animal will be captured and killed. Call it back while you still can."

"You will be amazed at how quickly the transforma-tion takes place. In less than an hour it will be able to fly, and we both will be away." An avaricious gleam formed in the sorcerer's eye. "And then the pair will mate and build their nest of gold." He sighed longingly. "Such a simple idea. I'm surprised no one thought of it before me."

"I guess the rest of us just don't have your creative mind."

"But to the matter at hand. You don't like my methods, you disagree with my goals, you've been chasing me for days, and you intend to kill or capture me, is that cor-rect?"

"Um, right."

"Fine, fine. I could kill you in an instant with my sword, and even more quickly with magic. But you ap-pear to be a rather bright young man. So I propose instead a test of wits."

He waited for Roland to make a sarcastic reply, which is usually what happens when anyone anywhere offers a test of wits. But Roland looked at the sorcerer specula-tively and seemed to be sizing him up, so the Middle-Aged Man of the Mountains went on. "You have heard of idogain extract?"

"No," said Roland, although he had.

The Middle-Aged Man of the Mountains took the vial from his pocket. It was a tiny bottle, half the length of his little finger, and half the width, stopped with a small cork. The remains of a wax seal still clung to the glass. He made an elaborate show of waving the bottle around, passing it from hand to hand, and holding it so lamplight shone through the red liquid inside. "The deadliest poison known to mankind. There is no antidote, nor can a person develop a tolerance for it. It can be taken orally, or absorbed through the skin. Death is immediate, which is very nice. You don't have to listen to all that whining and moaning about stomach cramps that you get with the vegetable alkaloids. And a single drop is enough to kill a man ten times over. So even though it is the rarest of poisons, and consequently very expensive, it is also economical."

"Because you don't need much."

"Exactly. The cost per victim is low, so you save money over the long run. I have mine imported by a specialty firm in Illyria. They bring it in by . . ."

"The test of wits," Roland prompted.

"Oh, right." The Middle-Aged Man of the Mountains waved his hand at the table. "You see these two glasses?"

Roland looked at the table. "I assume that's a rhetorical question."

"Don't be a smart aleck. One of them contains poison, and one does not. We will drink at the same time, although of course I will let you choose your glass first. The test, you see, is of your knowledge of people and the human mind. You must decide if I am the sort of person who will put the poison in the glass that is before his opponent or the glass before himself."

"And if I decline to drink?"

"We can fight it out with swords, and you are welcome to choose that option. But unless you have a great deal of confidence in your ability with the court sword, I'd advise you to try the glasses. At the very least, you have a fifty percent chance of survival."

Roland nodded. "That's a pretty convincing argument, sir."

The Middle-Aged Man of the Mountains winced slightly. "You don't have to call me 'sir.' I'm not yet old enough to be treated with respect."

"Sorry. It's just that you kind of remind me of my dad."

"Just pick a damn glass already!" the sorcerer snapped.

"Right," said Roland. Without hesitation he grabbed the glass nearest him and drained the contents, which tasted like scotch, in a single swallow. He coughed a little and slammed the glass back on the table. "Your turn."

He was surprised. He expected the Middle-Aged Man of the Mountains to come up with an excuse for not drinking. Or that the sorcerer would try some sort of trick. Perhaps he would pretend to spill the glass, or dash it in Roland's eyes and try to flee. Roland got ready to draw his sword again. But the sorcerer simply nodded, confidently picked up the other glass, held it toward Roland in a mock toast, and calmly drank it. He put the glass down, smiled at Roland, and said, "You are sur-prised?"

"Yes."

"Because you think I just drank the poison?"

"I know you did."

"And how do you know that, may I ask? Could it be

because you saw me add poison to this glass before you entered the room?"

The sorcerer saw the expression on Roland's face. "Yes, I knew you were skulking out there, watching me, before you kicked the door open. And therefore I drew your attention to the window. While you were looking outside, checking out the girls, I switched glasses."

"I know," said Roland. "I saw you switch them in the reflection from the glass window. So I picked the glass without the poison."

"I'm afraid not," said the Middle-Aged Man of Mountains. "I saw from the corner of my eye that you caught me switching them, so when you returned to the table I switched them back, with the help of a little misdirection. Your attention was diverted by the bottle of poison I was waving about."

Roland looked at the table doubtfully. "That doesn't seem right." He put his finger on one of the shot glasses. "You're saying the poison was in this glass?"

"No, the other one."

"But this is the one I drank from."

"No, you didn't. You drank from the one that is closest to you."

"Well sure, this one is closest to me now, because I put it down here. But when I picked it up, it was closer to you."

"Yes, I know that," the sorcerer said uncertainly. "I put the poison in the glass here, then I moved it to there when I switched them, then to here when I switched them back, then you picked up the glass that was—um—here. Right?"

"No, it was here. I think."

"Are you sure?"

"Um, no."

They both stood in silence for a minute, looking at the table with the two empty glasses. Roland picked up the bottle and sniffed it, then did the same to one of the glasses. "That won't do any good," said the Middle-Aged Man of the Mountains. "I already told you it was odorless."

"I know. I was just checking."

"Put the glass back in the same place! You're confusing things even more."

"Sorry."

"Okay, let's go over it again. You saw me put the poison in the glass here . . ."

"Wait," said Roland. "You said this stuff was supposed to be very fast. Instantly, you said. So, shouldn't one of us be dead by now?"

"It's always been fast before." The sorcerer checked his own pulse. "I feel fine."

"So do I. Let me see that poison again."

The Middle-Aged Man of the Mountains took the tiny bottle out of his pocket and passed it to Roland. Roland glanced at it. "Oh, for God's sake," he said with exasperation. "We've been waiting for nothing. This isn't idogain. It's *iodine!*"

"What!" The sorcerer grabbed the bottle back from him. "It's idogain." He looked closely at the label, then moved the bottle away from his face, then extended it a bit more, until finally he was holding it at arm's length, at the end of his fingertips, squinting at the small print.

"Iodine," Roland said firmly. "No wonder that drink tasted like scotch. You need to get reading glasses."

"I do not need reading glasses!" the Middle-Aged

Man of the Mountains shouted, dropping the vial on the table. He grabbed his sword again, brandishing it in such a threatening manner that Roland instinctively drew his own and backed into the center of the room. The sorcerer kicked the table over. Bottle and glasses shattered on the floor. The lamp went out. "All right, you young punk! You think you have the advantage of me in years? We'll see about that! You'll find out what skill and experience can do." Light from the palace came in through the windows, just enough to illuminate the sorcerer's face, his brows furrowed in anger. "Prepare to die!" The Middle-Aged Man of the Mountains pointed his sword at Roland's heart, and with a powerful, yet graceful leap, sprang over the couch.

Alison reached the top floor just in time to hear a loud cry of pain. She snapped the crossbow up to her shoulder and ran into the hallway, armed and ready to fire. Three soldiers of the Medullan army followed her, two with swords, the last with a mace. She saw the open door, and was about to rush into it, but one of the soldiers held her back. The other two went inside with their weapons ready. Nothing much happened. Alison could feel her heart beating against her ribs. Both soldiers came back out. One said to the other, "Get a medic. Tell him to bring a stretcher team."

"Oh!" was all Alison could say.

The soldier who spoke first told the third one, "The room is secure." He nodded and took a post by the door. The second soldier left to find a doctor. The first soldier took Alison by the arm and led her inside.

She was expecting the worst. She was not expecting to see Roland calmly standing in a corner of the room, his sword in his belt, looking down at the floor while he meticulously adjusted his cuffs. She let her crossbow drop to the floor while she ran and hugged him. "Roland! Are you all right? Where is the Middle-Aged Man of the Mountains? We heard him shouting while we were coming up the stairs. Did he get away?"

"Um, Miss?" said the soldier. "He's lying right at your feet, Miss."

Alison looked down. "Oh, right." The Middle-Aged Man of the Mountains was flat on his back, looking up at her. She wondered why she hadn't noticed him before. He was still alive, but his teeth were clenched, and his face was twisted into an expression of pure anguish.

"Come on," said Roland. He took Alison's arm. "The king's men will take care of him from here on. Right, gentlemen?" The soldiers nodded. "Let's go and find the others." He led her into the hall and closed the door. "But first, another kiss."

"Good idea," said Alison, and did the job thoroughly, putting her tongue into play and backing it up with lots of body language. When they finally pulled away from each other she said, "But Roland, what happened in there?"

"I tried to capture him. I gave him a chance to surrender. He attacked me."

"What did you do? Did you stab him? I didn't see any blood. Did you beat him up?"

Roland seemed reluctant to speak. He seemed to be wrestling with his conscience. It wasn't until they reached the ground floor, and walked out into the night air, that he put his arm around her waist and said, "In all honesty,

Alison, I didn't do anything. I never touched him, in fact. He threw his back out jumping over the couch."

Alison rested her head on his chest and laughed. "Of course."

Gloria ran through the hallways, following a smell of smoke and singed feathers, in hot pursuit of the enraged gryphon. She had only caught a glimpse of it, but it was easy to follow. Its giant claws left marks on the hardwood floor, and its massive shoulders knocked the paintings from the walls. It was also insanely suicidal to follow it, but Gloria was past caring, or even thinking about danger. The excitement of the chase, the hazardous ride, and stress of the last week had caught up with her. She was dizzy and disoriented from lack of food and sleep, and the only thing she felt at this point was guilt.

It's my fault, she thought. *The gryphon wouldn't be here if not for my plan. All the danger is because of me. Now I have to stop it.* She gripped the sword more tightly and forced herself to run faster.

Ahead of her the gryphon, maddened by pain, was screeching angrily. The hallway had cleared. The doors on both sides were shut and bolted, the inhabitants cowering within. She thought she could even hear the sound of furniture being piled against the doors. She rounded a corner, and the beast, at long last, came into her sight. It reached the end of the hall, which had a sitting nook with a large bay window. The gryphon stopped, perhaps confused by its own reflection in the glass. It looked back over its shoulder, gave her one contemptuous glance, then burst through the wood frame and into the open air. Spicules of glass rained on the floor. Gloria covered her eyes.

Incredibly, no one else saw it.

Gloria stepped out through the window. The lacemakers were gathered across the courtyard. They were looking the other way, toward a handful of dressmakers who were standing in the back of an open carriage, arguing about prices. Other people were moving hastily along the sidewalks, intent on where they were going, their ears muffled by hats and scarves. Music was coming from somewhere. Snack vendors were absorbed with setting up their carts, trying to get their stoves lit. The palace loomed to one side. Gloria could see figures moving behind the brightly lit windows, but none seemed to be looking out. All seemed to be oblivious to the danger bounding across the cobbles.

It's up to me, thought Gloria, and she tried to call out to the girls, but she had been running too hard. She no longer had the breath to make herself heard above the music and the street noise. She slipped on a wet cobblestone, fell painfully onto her knees, and used the sword to push herself back up. Her legs hurt, but she kept running, even though she knew she was too late. Too late to stop the carnage that the gryphon was about to unleash.

Except that, miraculously, the gryphon stopped.

It went into a crouch, held the pose for a moment, and started moving again. The massive beak opened slightly. The wings were once again flattened along its back, and it kept its body low to the ground as it crept forward, slowly, silently, and deliberately, turning its head from side to side to keep its quarry in view.

It's stalking, thought Gloria. *Like a giant feathered cat.* It seemed ridiculous that a creature as big as a gryphon would try to remain unnoticed, and it seemed equally impossible that the people in the square could continue to not notice it. But the girls on the street were absorbed in their haggling, and the boys on the street were absorbed in the girls. The gryphon moved into pouncing range. It gathered itself into a knot of muscle and malice, then tensed, about to spring like a robin on a worm. But it had delayed just enough for Gloria to reach it. There was nothing for her to do but run right up to the beast and plunge the sword into its rear.

That got its attention. That got everyone's attention. The gryphon let out a screech that froze the blood of everyone for six blocks around. Heads turned on the street. Mouths dropped open. Bands stopped. Horse bolted, sending their carriages careening up the sidewalk. In the palace the servants and courtiers ran to the windows. In the treetops the birds that had settled down for the night suddenly rose and filled the air with their fluttering. In the streets the rats disappeared into the sewers. The girls in the square screamed, dropped their lace, and scattered.

And in the courtyard the gryphon turned, lifted one giant paw, and flattened Gloria against the frozen stones.

The blow left her stunned, and fear left her paralyzed, unable even to scream, trapped within giant claws that surrounded her like a cage. The gryphon crouched over her and gave another earsplitting screech. It nearly deafened her. The beast wasn't hungry, at least not for her, but it was certainly mad. It bent its head low and looked at her with an eye that was as big as a saucer and black as espresso. It opened its beak, that giant curved meat hook of a beak, capable of biting her in two with a single snap, and lowered it for the kill. It was about to close its jaws on her when Terry split its head open with an ax.

It collapsed right away. It took quite a bit of straining, even for Terry, to roll it off the Princess and help her to her feet, where she clung unsteadily to him. When she was finally able to talk, she said, "Terry, where were you?"

"Right behind you the whole time. I called out, but you didn't hear. But, you know, honey?" Terry paused to survey the comatose gryphon. "Maybe you ought to let me slay the monsters from now on. At least until you get more experience."

"Right. Good job, by the way."

"I couldn't have done it without you. Excuse me." Terry set Gloria on her feet, whereupon he took the ax and proceeded to separate the gryphon's head from its body. He did a neat and workmanlike job of it, then tossed the ax aside and collected Gloria for another kiss. "When magic is involved, it's always a good idea to remove the head." Around them the girls were filtering back to look at the decapitated monster. Above them, every light in the palace seemed to be on, and the windows were thrown open so the inhabitants could hang their heads out and look down. Even the king and queen appeared on a balcony.

Gloria seized the moment.

She threw herself against the knight. "My hero!" she yelled at the top of her voice. "You have saved me!" Everyone—the girls in the square, the men on the street, the faces in the windows, and especially her parents on

the balcony, fixed their eyes on Gloria—but for the bene-
fit of any dullards who might be among the witnesses, she
also added, "*My rescuer!*" And then she proceeded to
swoon in Terry's arms.

"What was that all about?" Terry said.

"Look up," Gloria whispered with her eyes closed.
"Try to look heroic."

Terry looked up. He saw that the windows were lined
with officers, court officials, and Medullan nobility.
"Right," he said, and struck his best heroic pose. "How's
this?"

"It will do," murmured the Princess. She let her eyes
open a slit. Above her she could see the queen, looking
very angry. Gloria smiled.

"Men!" said the princess in exasperation.
"You're all the same. Oh sure, you're quick enough with
the words of endearment, with the loving notes, and the
little gifts. You tell us how much we mean to you and that
we're the most important thing in your lives. But the truth
is, deep down inside, all you really want is one thing."

Terry thought for a minute. "Free beer?"

"Exactly."

They were sitting in an upstairs parlor of a recently re-
named tavern called The Great Gryphon. It had a bay
window, a sideboard, and a collection of overstuffed
chairs and sofas. A small fire burned in the grate. Outside,
a light dusting of new snow covered the streets. Two
weeks had passed since Gloria's "rescue." At that time
the tavern had been called The Gray Goat, and the stuffed
head of a mountain ram had been mounted over the big

fireplace in the main saloon. Now the stuffed head of the gryphon had taken its place.

"Free beer for life," said Terry, explaining the deal he had made with the owner in exchange for the head. "We can have some right now, if you want."

"Yuck, no. It's still only midmorning. We will stick with tea, thank you very much." Gloria was setting out the tea service on the sideboard.

"It's only girls who come up with things like proper times for drinking."

"Oh yes? Well, girls come up with things like this, too." Gloria launched herself at Terry and knocked him back onto a sofa. She climbed on top of him and began kissing him all over his face. "What do think of this, big guy?"

"Don't start anything," warned Terry, between kisses. "They'll be here any moment."

"Start something? Me? Whose idea was it to put his hand up my dress, hmmm? Who decided it was okay to touch me—ooooh—there? Hmmm? Hmmm?"

They had just emerged from a meeting of the Royal Council, where the king and the queen had finally, and officially, sanctioned their marriage. It had been a grueling two weeks, especially for Terry. He had been suspended without pay from the Royal Guard, questioned again and again, detained for hours while various government officials threatened him with prosecution, held in a small cell while high-ranking officers took turns shouting at him, and eventually released with multiple warnings not to leave the city. Through it all he stuck to the new story Gloria had concocted, but the next day he was ordered to report for another interview, and the questioning began all over again. The third day started out with more of the same until, to his astonishment, a lawyer named Miligras showed up, announced he was representing Terry's case, and declared that all further questions would be submitted through his office.

After that things went smoothly. Terry was reinstated with back pay. Miligras demanded a hearing before the Royal Council. There he quickly proved that the tradition of awarding a girl's hand in marriage to a knight who rescued her from mortal danger had the force of law. Indeed, he was able to cite precedents going all the way back to the days of Queen Donna the Wannabe. Gloria's mother objected. She insisted that the law applied to dragons, not to gryphons. Miligras was prepared for this. With the aid of illustrated flip charts, he convinced the council that dragons, gryphons, and kidnappers were the same for legal purposes. The expert witness brought in by the Westfield family flubbed his testimony, apparently thrown off-balance by Miligras' expert cross-examination, or perhaps the numerous sharp glances from Gloria. The fact that the princess had obtained for his wife a coveted invitation to the royal New Year's Eve party was never mentioned.

Now they had only to wait for Roland and Alison to arrive before they would celebrate. When they stopped kissing long enough to catch their breath, Terry wondered aloud how the other two were getting along. "I don't know if it's a good thing when a relationship starts out with a deception."

"You knights are too honorable for your own good," said Gloria. "Our relationship is based on a massive deception."

"Yes, but we were deceiving other people. We didn't

deceive each other." He saw Gloria looking at him thoughtfully. "Gloria, promise me that after we're married, you will never lie to me."

Gloria laid a hand on his arm. "Sweetie, I promise that if I ever find it necessary to deceive you, I will make it up to you with lots and lots of really hot sex."

Terry thought this over. "Yeah, okay. That's better than what I was asking for anyway."

That kicked off another bout of kissing, which was interrupted by a gentle rap on the door. "Are you decent?" asked Alison's voice. "Get your clothes back on."

Gloria quickly adjusted her dress. "Come in."

The door opened. The room quickly filled with the smell of freshly baked bread. Roland and Alison came in, each with a large basket of bread, rolls, muffins, and tea cakes, which they set on the sideboard next to the tea service. Alison was wearing all new clothes, courtesy of Gloria's wardrobe. Roland was wearing a long cashmere coat that had been custom-tailored to his lean figure. Terry had to admit that he looked extremely sharp but couldn't help noticing that the flour on his cuffs sort of ruined the effect. Roland and Alison had been spending a lot of time in Roland's shop, trying out recipes.

"So how did it go?" he asked Roland.

"They cut me off without a penny," Roland said cheerfully.

"No! Really?"

"Your father sent this to you," Gloria told Alison, presenting her with a long, slim object wrapped in brown paper. Alison tore off the wrapper, revealing a black iron fork with a long handle.

"Oh good. I've been waiting for this. You know, on the

bright side, at least my father is off the hook for the kidnapping. It never even came up in the hearing."

"It always was the harshest part of the original plan," Gloria admitted. "But Miligras is a good lawyer. I remember I once sat in on a case where he argued that up was down. When the jury let out, half of them took the wrong stairs."

"What are you doing?" said Roland. "What is that?"

"It's a toasting fork," Alison said, holding it up proudly. "I invented it. It's for toasting sliced bread."

Roland made a face, but before he could say anything, Terry picked up the thread again. "Your family disowned you? Why? Surely they understand that it wasn't your fault?"

"They were furious. They were counting heavily on me marrying into the royal family. They said I didn't try hard enough. They said I should have killed the gryphon myself. Even my father was mad."

"My own father has many faults," said Alison, "but I must admit he never asked me to kill monsters." She switched her attention to Gloria. "Did you bring butter and jam?"

"In the small pots."

"Dad said it was nothing to be afraid of," Roland continued. "It's just a giant bird with claws, he said. I don't think he really took a good look at it."

"Maybe they'll calm down after a while."

Roland shook his head. "To hell with them. Alison and I talked it over and decided we will make it on our own. I'm not too proud to work. And I have a gentleman's education. I can get some sort of clerical job. We don't need a lot of money to be happy."

"Right," said Alison, waving a freshly browned piece of toast for emphasis. "I'll go back to work, too. We'll get by. And you know, without Count Bussard putting the screws to us all the time, eventually the debt on my father's estate will be paid off."

"Of course we'll be old and gray by then," said Roland.

"So we'll have a nice place to retire to."

Terry exchanged looks with Gloria, trying to decide if he should speak first. She gave him a nod, so he said, "Roland? Alison?" He cleared his throat. "Um, we kind of expected that something like that might happen, so Gloria has a plan."

"*We* have a plan," Gloria corrected him.

"Right. *We* have a plan, but I'll let Gloria tell you about it."

"It turned out there was a bounty for killing the gryphon," said Gloria. "It falls into the classification of 'marauding varmint.' It isn't a great deal of money, but Terry and I decided that the four of us will split it, since the whole pursuit was a group effort."

"That's very generous of you both," Roland began. "But we don't need . . ."

"There's a need for a new baker in Middleton," continued Gloria. "We're going to be moving there. The old baker told us he wants to retire. He's putting his place up for sale. So we thought, why don't we all use the bounty money for a down payment on the bakery. Then you and Alison could bake there."

"We should check this out, Roland." Alison carefully spread a pat of butter across her toast. "I've often thought that the workers should own the means of production."

"You can make anything you want," added Gloria. "You could make that bread with the seeds."

"I like the rye bread with seeds," said Terry.

"What are you eating?" asked Roland.

Alison had to chew and swallow before she could answer. "Toasted bread with butter and jam. Do you want some?" She held the piece up to Roland. He took it and looked at it carefully.

"You put butter and jam on toasted bread?"

Alison nodded. "It's something we started doing at the inn. People think that toasted bread is safer to eat, but the problem is that toasting the bread makes it dry. So we started putting butter on it, and then we added jam for breakfast and tea. Everyone loves it."

Roland took a bite of the toast. He chewed it slowly and thoughtfully. His eyes got wide. He took another bite.

"See, I noticed that people were dipping their toast in their tea. Also their coffee. So I tried spraying it with water, using a plant mister. But the customers complained that they didn't want soggy toast, even though they made it soggy when they dunked it. Go figure. Anyway, the butter and jam was a big hit. We sell pots of it every morning. It was my idea," Alison finished proudly.

"Mmmph," said Roland. He swallowed. "Alison," he said, quietly and seriously. He knelt next to her chair. "I want you think carefully about your next answer. Are you absolutely certain that you thought of this all by yourself?"

"Oh yes," said Alison. "Everyone thinks it's a crazy idea until they try it for the first time. It only works with sliced bread, too. If you try it with broken bread, it won't toast evenly."

"And," said Roland, still outwardly calm, "did you think to patent the idea?"

"Well, no. It's just a simple recipe. Kind of silly, really."

"Patent it!" said Roland. He stood up abruptly. "Tomorrow! We'll draw up the patent today, and you can file it first thing tomorrow. Yes!" He snapped his fingers. "Toasted bread with butter and jam." He turned to Gloria and Terry. "We'll need some of that bounty money for the filing fees."

"No problem," said Gloria.

Roland began pacing back and forth, brainstorming out loud, waving the toast around as he spoke. "Jam. We'll need jam. No. We don't buy the jam. We'll buy options on future jam production. Someone take notes." Terry scrambled to find ink and a quill. "Strawberry," Roland said. "Grape. Raspberry, blackberry, and apple. And that other stuff. Not apple jelly, the brown stuff."

"Apple butter!" said Alison, getting caught up in Roland's excitement. "Marmalade!"

"Right. Apple butter. Anything that can be spread on toasted bread."

"Yeast paste," offered Gloria.

"Say what?" said Terry.

"That stuff from the bottom of brewers' vats."

"Who would eat that? It tastes like burned grease"

"It's good for you," Gloria insisted.

"Write it down," said Roland. "We'll patent the toasting fork also. Of course at first we'll just give them away."

"We will not!" Alison clutched her fork. "I invented this."

"It's called a loss leader, my love," said Roland. "It

will help build the market for toasted bread with jam." He ate the rest of the toast while he thought. "We'll take out two patents. One specifically for the toasting fork, and then another general patent to try to cover all possible bread-toasting equipment—the toasting fork, the toasting knife, the toasting spoon, the toasting corkscrew. Whatever you can think of."

"Okay."

"I'll develop a business plan, then we'll get to work rounding up investors. They won't be a problem." He picked Alison out of her chair, spun her around, and hugged her. "When word gets out that we're partnered with a princess and a knight, people will be flocking to invest with us."

Gloria and Terry looked at each other. Simultaneously, they both shrugged. "I'm in," said Gloria.

"Me too," said Terry.

"Roland," said Alison. "Do you really think this will work?"

"Toasted bread with butter and jam," said Roland. He kissed her. "Darling, this is going to be big."